THE BAITAL PACHISI

TWENTY FIVE GHOST STORIES

THE BAITAL PACHISI

TWENTY FIVE GHOST STORIES

translated by
CAPTAIN W. HOLLINGS

PILGRIMS PUBLISHING
◆ Varanasi ◆

THE BAITAL PACHISI: Twenty-five Ghost Stories
Translated by **CAPTAIN W. HOLLINGS**

Published by:
PILGRIMS PUBLISHING

An imprint of:
PILGRIMS BOOK HOUSE
(Distributors in India)
B 27/98 A-8, Nawabganj Road
Durga Kund, Varanasi-221010, India
Tel: 91-542-2314059, 2314060, 2312456
Fax: 91-542-2312788, 2311612
E-mail: pilgrims@satyam.net.in
Website: www.pilgrimsbooks.com

PILGRIMS BOOK HOUSE (New Delhi)
9 Netaji Subhash Marg, 2nd Floor
Near Neeru Hotel,
Daryaganj,
New Delhi 110002
Tel: 91-11-23285081
E-mail: pilgrim@del2.vsnl.net.in

Distributed in Nepal by:
PILGRIMS BOOK HOUSE
P O Box 3872, Thamel,
Kathmandu, Nepal
Tel: 977-1-4424942
Fax: 977-1-4424943
E-mail: pilgrims@wlink.com.np

First Edition 1910, M. L. Bhargava at the Newul Kishore Press

ISBN: 81-7769-116-3
Rs.

Cover Design by Sasya
Layout by Asha
Edited by Bob Gibbons and Sian Pritchard-Jones with Christopher N Burchett

Printed in India

CONTENTS

PREFACE TO THE NEW EDITION

First published in 1848 and reprinted in 1910, this book is a translation of some of the traditional stories of Indian and Hindu mythology told long-long ago, in an era that will never again be experienced.

Before reading this book, one might be well advised to look a little deeper into Hindu mythology and examine some of the stories associated with India's great epic tales. Although many of the parables told relate to Hindu mythology, their underlying meaning will be all too readily familiar to all. The tales that are told here bring to life and illustrate some of the great truths about the notions and nature of humankind.

The messages that the stories carry come through the medium of the Baital. A Baital is a mythical evil-sprit who is said to have had great power. He is a wraith-like figure who can enter the body of a deceased and bring life to that body for a short time.

Some of the stories give an underlying moral teaching. Others are far more human and a trifle more subtle. Some stories will perhaps baffle you, and you will need to seek a greater or simpler meaning to appreciate the underlying lesson. Others will entertain and bring humour and mirth to your face.

As we republish these tales of old, nearly 150 years have passed, but are any of the meanings less diminished than when they were first told?

PREFACE TO THE TRANSLATION
OF THE
BAITAL PACHISI

My object in translating this work, the Baital Pachisi, has been to produce a translation which might enable the youngest Officer in the Army, commencing the study of the Hindi and Hindustani languages, to enter upon the study with a confident assurance, that while reading the work he understood all that he was reading.

Beginners are too apt to be discouraged from prosecuting the study of the languages by the difficulties they meet with at first, and by not understanding the explanations of their Munshis and Pundits. I have, therefore, endeavoured to make this translation a very literal one.

The Baital Pachisi is a compound of Hindi and Hindustani, with more Hindi than Hindustani; but still containing many Persian, and Arabic words.

It is also an examination book, I believe at all the three Presidencies of the army; and, therefore, I thought that a translation might not be unacceptable for the use of beginners.

I now proceed to give a few hints and brief suggestions for the study of the native languages.

First of all, I cannot too strongly impress upon the mind of the young student, that a study of grammar is the primary and most essential requisite. I do not mean the niceties of grammar, but the rudiments the declension of nouns, adjectives, and the pronouns, the conjugation of verbs, and the elementary parts of syntax.

Some persons have an opinion that it is not necessary to begin with grammar; that to do so impedes a student's progress; and that a man studying can pick up the grammar, as he progresses in the language. But this seems to me like putting the cart before the horse.

Would anyone think that of attempting to solve a problem of Euclid, until he had first made himself acquainted with the definitions and axioms? And why then attempt to translate a sentence, until you know what a noun, pronoun, or verb, is and how they act and react upon each other? Another mistake often made is to suppose, that a good colloquial linguist or "bolee man" (a term I have often heard applied to a person who has the reputation of speaking the language well, but has never studied it) speaks better, and can make himself better understood by the natives, than passed interpreters, and men who have studied.

Now I have met with many gentlemen who had this reputation, but I confess that I never in my life saw one who had attained that most essential quality in a linguist—*correctness*. It is of little avail to be master, if mistakes are constantly made in the construction of sentences and wrong cases, wrong tenses, and wrong idioms constantly employed. I repeat, therefore, that it is most essential for a student to begin with the grammar, which is in fact the key of a language, and, without a knowledge of which, no one can hope to be a sound or proficient scholar.

And now for a few hints as to the study of grammar I recommend Shakespeare's Hindustani grammar to the student. Let him begin with the alphabet in the Persian and Devanagari characters, which he should learn by heart, and frequently write out, so as to become thoroughly acquainted with the letters. Then the remarks regarding the short vowels and other orthographical signs should be read attentively, and also the remarks regarding the combination and pronunciation to letters. These remarks need not be committed to memory, but an attentive perusal of them will be found very useful. Chapter the third on the noun, the fourth on the pronoun, and the fifth on the verb, should be studied most thoroughly, and committed to memory.

These three chapters are most important, and contain about five-sixths of the amount of rudimentary knowledge required by a student.

I would suggest that the nouns be written out both in the Persian and Devanagari characters in all their cases, as they are written in the Hindustani Brajbhasa grammar, supplied by the Government to each native regiment: and the verb should be written out, in like manner, in both characters, in all their tenses, and in the active and passive voices.

The sixth chapter on indeclinable word, the seventh on the numerals, and the eighth, on derivative words need not be read until the students has made some progress in the language. I recommend the whole of the syntax being read over most carefully three or four times.

And this is the whole of the rudimentary parts of grammar,

which I recommend the beginner to study; the niceties and other more difficult parts he can study, when he has made some progress in the languages.

But this extent of knowledge, which I think a student of ability might acquire in two months, so as to have it imprinted indelibly upon his memory, will enable a beginner to enter upon his reading with great confidence, and he will have no difficulty in knowing what part of a verb, or what part of a noun, such and such a word is, and how certain words are compounded.

The above extent of grammar having been acquired I next suggested the reading and translating a few easy fables, say ten or twelve, such as those contained in the first volume of Hindustani Selections.

The translations should be made very literally, and be written out and rules of grammar should be brought most strictly into play; in fact, every word should be analyzed and parsed.

And after some days, the English translations should be rendered back into the Native language, by the aid of *Dictionary and Grammar* and compared with the originals, when all errors should be corrected and all sentences of peculiar construction, all idiomatic phrases, and all points denoting the nature and genius of the language, and differing from English idioms and constructions, be carefully remarked. The student can then proceed to read the Baital Pachisi, and afterwards the Prem Sagar, Bagh-o-Bahar, and Gulistan pursuing, with respect of these works, the same system of translation analysis and parsing.

This may appear to some a laborious mode of studying languages; but I am convinced, from a long experience, that it is a simple and easy one; and that a fair trial of this mode being made, difficulties will be found to vanish more quickly than could be imagined. I cannot think of any other method of studying a language, by means of which the great object (correctness) can be so well attained.

Many men may perhaps become tolerably good linguists by other processes of studying the grammar, and analyzing each sentence; at first, no one can be a correct one. With respect to correct pronunciation, it is scarcely possible to give rule, as English, Irish, and Scotchmen pronounce all languages differently from each other; and, in point of fact, there seems to be no rule for the pronunciation of any language, except the custom of the country:—

"Utvolet usus,
Quem pens arbitrium et jus, et norma loquendi"

The best suggestion I can offer is to employ good Munshis and Pundits, listen attentively to their reading and accent, and endeavour to adopt their pronunciation.

The books which will be found useful, in addition to the four examination books, are Shakespeare's Hindustani Dictionary (an invaluable work), the two volumes of Hindi and Hindustani Selections, furnished by the Government of Regiments, Gilchrist's Dialogues, and Captain Starkey's Interpreter, which contains many military terms and phrases, useful to Officers on occasions of duty.

There are also some good dialogues and military terms and phrases in the selections and Gilchrist's work. Frequent conversations with all classes of natives, Munshis, Pundits, gentlemen of rank, native officers and sepoys, give a student great colloquial readiness and facility, and the characters, manners, and customs of orientals.

The young officer cannot employ a portions of his leisure time better, than in conversing freely and unreservedly with the native officers and men, not merely on points of duty, but also on their private affairs, which the more respectable portion of the men, who look up to their officers for advice and protection, will not hesitate to lay before him. By this means not only will he improve in his colloquial knowledge, but will acquire for himself the attachment of the sepoys, founded on the high estimation they will have formed of his character.

W. Hollings, *Captain*,
47th Regiment

Naini Tal
11th July, 1848.

THE BAITAL PACHISI

There was once a city named Dharanagar, and its King was called Gandharb Sen. He had four queens, and by them six sons, each of whom was more learned and more powerful that the other.

When the King died, his eldest son, named Shank, succeeded him as King. After some time Vikram, his younger brother, having killed his elder brother, became King and began to govern well.

Day by day his dominion increased, until he became King of the whole of India. He created a stable government and established a good era.

Sometime after this, the King thought that he ought to visit some other countries. Having decided this, he gave up his throne to his younger brother, Bhartaree. He then become a devotee (yogi), and began to wander through different countries and forests.

Now a certain Brahmin in the city was practising austere devotion. One day a god presented to him the fruit of immortality, which the Brahmin took home. He said to his wife, "Whosoever shall eat this shall be immortal; this is what the divinity told me when he presented the fruit to me."

When the Brahmin's wife heard this she wept much. She said, "It has fallen to our lot to suffer the punishment of a great crime, because if we become immortal, to what indefinite period of time shall we beg? It would be better to die than to ask for alms for so long. If we were to die, we would escape from the afflictions of the world."

The Brahmin replied, "I have received and brought the fruit here; but my understanding has been destroyed by hearing what you have said; I will now do whatever you say."

His wife answered, "Give the fruit to the King and receive wealth in exchange, in order that you may be able to perform acts of religious merit yourself and promote religious merit to others."

Having heard this, the Brahmin went to the King and gave him his blessing. After having explained all the circumstances connected with the fruit, he said, "O great king! Be pleased to accept the fruit, and bestow some riches upon me. I shall be made happy by your living long."

The King gave the Brahmin one lakh of rupees and allowed him to leave. He then came to the female apartments and, having given the fruit to the queen whom he loved most, said "O queen eat this, that you may be immortal, and be perpetually young."

The queen, having heard this speech, received the fruit from the King. She then gave the fruit to a Kotwal, who gave it to a prostitute, a friend of his. He explained its qualities.

The prostitute thought to herself that the fruit was a fit present for the King. She gave the fruit to the King, who accepted it, and bestowed great wealth upon her and permitted her to take leave.

Having looked at the fruit, and reflected in his mind, he was dissatisfied with the world, and began to say, "The wealth of this world is of no use, because in consequence of it, we fall hereafter into hell. For which reason it is better to practice religious austerities and to hold Bhagwan in remembrance, in order that it may be good for us in future."

Having formed this resolution he went to his wives and asked the queen what she had done with the fruit he had given her. She said that she had eaten it. The KIng then showed the fruit to the queen, who, on seeing it, stood aghast and was unable to reply.

After this, the King had the fruit washed, ate it and abandoned his government and throne. He became a devotee (yogi) and went alone into the forest.

The government of Vikram remained without a head. When news of this reached King Indra, he sent a demon to guard Dharanagar, who kept watch over the city day and night.

At length it was heard abroad from country to country, how King Bhartaree had abandoned his government, and gone forth into the jungle. When King Vikram heard the news he returned immediately to his own country. It was then midnight but, while he was going into the city, the demon that was guarding it called out, "Who are you, and where are you going? Stop and tell me your name!"

The King said, "I am King Vikram, and I am going into my own city; who are you, that stops me?" The demon replied, "The gods have send me to protect this city; if you are really King Vikram, first fight with me and then go into the city.

On hearing these words, the King challenged the demon. The fight began; at length the King, having thrown the demon down, sat on his chest.

He said, "King! You have thrown me down; I therefore grant you your life."

Then the King said laughing. "You must be mad, to whom do you grant life? If I wished, I could put you to death; how will you grant me life?"

The demon replied, "King! I will save you from death; listen first to what I am about to say, and afterwards rule over the whole world free from all care." At length, the King let go his hold on him and began to listen in earnest to what he said.

The demon said to him, "There was in this city a very liberal King, named Chandra Bhan. By chance he went forth one day into the jungle, and saw there a devotee suspended from a tree, with his head downwards, and constantly inhaling smoke. He did not receive anything from anyone, nor did he speak to anyone. Having seen him in this state, the King came home and having sat down in his court, said, "If anyone will bring this devotee here, he shall receive one lakh of rupees." Having heard this, a courtesan came to the King and solicited him; "If I obtain your highness's permission, I will, after having had a child by the devotee, bring it here riding on his shoulders."

The King was astonished at this speech and, having given the courtesan betel, allowed her to depart. She went to the forest and, having arrived at the devotee's abode, saw that he really was really suspended with his head downwards; he ate nothing and drank nothing and was withered.

At length the courtesan, having prepared some confections, put them into the devotee's mouth, which licked them up. She then put more sweetmeats into his mouth, which he also ate with relish. In this manner, for two days she made him taste sweet-meats. From eating he gained strength. He then opened his eyes, and descended from the tree and asked her, "For what purpose have you come here?" The courtesan said, "I am the daughter of a god, I used to practice religious austerities in the celestial regions, and have now come into this forest." The devotee then said, "Show me where your hut is." The courtesan, having brought the devotee to her hut, began to have all sorts of delicacies prepared for him, so that he gave up inhaling smoke and began to eat and drink daily. At length, Cupid troubled him, and he had connection with the courtesan, who became pregnant. In ten months a male child was born.

When he was some months old, the woman said to the devotee, 'O holy saint! Be pleased to go now and perform a pilgrimage, by means of which all the sins of your body will be effaced. Having deceived him with this speech, and placed the child on his shoulders, she went to the King's court from where she had come. When she came into the King's presence, he recognised her from a distance and, having seen the child on the devotee's shoulder, began to say to the people of the assembly, "Behold! This is the courtesan who went to bring the devotee."

They said, "O great king! You speak truly; this is the person whom you mention, and be pleased to observe, that all the matters have been accomplished."

When the devotee heard these speeches of the King and of the courtiers, he imagined that the King had adopted these measures for the purpose of interrupting his austere devotion. With these thoughts in his mind, he went outside the city, killed the child, and began to perform penance in a jungle. After some days, the King's death occurred and the yogi completed his penance.

"You three were born in the same city, the same mansion of the moon, the same division of the great circle and the same period of time equal to two gharees, or forty-eight minutes. You were born in a King's house; the second was born in the house of an oilman; and the third, the devotee, in the house of a potter. You govern here, and the oilman's son was master of the government. The potter having performed his penance well, killed the oilman, and metamorphosed him into an evil spirit in a cemetery. He has kept him suspended with his head downward from a sirus tree, and is thinking to kill you also. If you escape from him, you shall have royal power. I have informed you of these circumstances. Do not be careless in regard to them."

When the demon had spoken thus, he went away. The Rajah went to his seraglio. In the morning, having come forth, he sat down, and gave an order for a general court. All his servants came to him and offered presents, and musical rejoicing was heard. The whole city were greatly delighted and overjoyed; in every house there was dancing and singing.

After this, the King began to govern justly. It so happened that one day a devotee, named Shant Sheel, came into the King's court with a fruit in his hand. Having given it to the King, and spread a cloth on the ground, he sat down. After about a quarter of an hour the King thought to himself this may be the person of whom the demon spoke. Suspecting this he did not eat the fruit and, having called the steward of his household, gave it to him, and told him to keep it carefully. But the devotee came each day and gave the King a fruit daily.

By chance the King went one day to see his stable with some companions. In the meantime the devotee came there and, as usual, put a fruit into the King's hand. The King began to toss it in the air, when all of a sudden it fell on the ground and a monkey broke it into pieces. A ruby of such brilliant quality came from it that the King and his companions were astonished.

The King then said to the devotee, "Why have you given me this ruby?"

He replied, "O great king! It is written in the Shastra, that we ought not to go empty-handed to a King, spiritual preceptor, astrologer, physician or young girl, because giving presents to them is profitable. King! Why do you mention only a single ruby? There is a jewel in every one of the fruits I have given you."

Having heard this, the King said to his steward, "Bring all the fruits. The steward brought them immediately and found a ruby in each fruit, which he split.

The King was exquisitely pleased to behold so many rubies. He summoned a jeweller and had the rubies proved and saying, "Nothing shall go with anyone after death, so tell with truth and integrity, the value of each jewel."

Having heard these words, the jewellers said "O great king! You have spoken truly. He, whose integrity remains, is possessed of everything. Integrity is with us and is of advantage in both worltds. O great king! Hear me, each gem is perfect in colour, quality and appearance. If I were to pronounce the value of each to be one crore of rupees it would not be enough. In truth each jewel is equal in value to a seventh of the world.

The King was greatly pleased and having bestowed honour on the jeweller allowed him to take leave. He took the devotee by the hand and seated him on a throne and began to say, "My whole country is not equal in price to one of these rubies; please explain what is the reason that you, who are naked, have given me so many jewels?"

The devotee said, "It is not proper to talk publicly of enchantments, incantations, family circumstances and any evil that we may have heard of anyone. These things are not spoken of in public; I will speak of them in private. It is the way of the world that what is heard by three people, cannot be kept secret. No one hears what transpires between two persons.

The King, on hearing these words and having taken the devotee aside, began to say, "O holy saint! I am greatly ashamed that you should not have once eaten food. Tell me what you desire."

The devotee answered, "King! I will practice enchantments where bodies are burnt on the bank of the river at Godavari. My purpose will be completely successful, and all my objects accomplished. I ask only from you that you remain one night with me. By your remaining near me, my incantations will be successful."

The King then said, "Go away now, I will certainly come along."

Having thus exacted a promise from the King, he went into the temple and made preparations. He then proceeded to the place where bodies were burnt and sat down. The King also began to meditate upon what had taken place.

The King, girding his sword and fastening tight the cloth he wore between his legs, went alone in the night to the devotee and saluted him. The devotee (*Yogi*) invited him to come and sit down. And when he had done so, the King beheld on all sides different kinds of ghosts and spectres, and witches, who had assumed frightful forms, dancing, and the *Yogî* seated in the midst of them, playing on two skulls.

The King was not at all afraid or alarmed, and said to the devotee, "What orders do you have for me?"

He said, "King, since you have come here, do one thing. Where the bodies are burnt, there is a sirus tree, and on it is a suspended corpse. Bring it to me, while I perform my devotions here."

Having sent off the King, the yogi sat on the ground and began to repeat prayers.

The darkness of the night was terrible, and the rain poured down with great violence. Unclean sprits were making such a noise and uproar those even brave and resolute men would have been perplexed on beholding them; but the King pursued his journey. Snakes kept twisting themselves around his legs but by pronouncing incantations he made them loosen themselves. At length, when the King arrived at the place where they burnt bodies, he saw that goblins were laying hold of and eating men. Witches were chewing the livers of children; tigers were roaring and elephants screaming. When he cast his eyes on the tree he saw, that from the root to the topmost twig, every branch and leaf was ablaze; and on every side there were confused cries of "Kill! Kill! Seize him! Seize! Take care that he does not escape."

The King was not afraid but said to himself; "this must certainly be the yogi of whom the demon spoke to me." Going nearer, he saw a corpse fastened by a rope and hanging with its head downwards. He was pleased at seeing the corpse. Taking his sword and shield, he fearlessly climbed the tree and struck the rope so forcibly with his sword that it broke. The corpse fell to the ground and, while falling began to cry violently. On hearing the sound of his lamentations, the King was delighted, and began to say to himself, "This man must be alive." Having descended from the tree, he enquired who he was.

On hearing these words the corpse burst out laughing. The King was greatly astonished and the corpse climbed the tree again, becoming suspended as before. The King went up the tree without any delay and pressing the corpse under his arm brought it down with him and said, "Vile wretch! Tell me who you are."

He made no reply. The King, having reflected, said to himself, "This is perhaps the oilman of whom the demon said that the yogi kept him confined in a place where bodies were burnt."

With these thoughts in his mind, the Rajah fastened him in his cloth and brought him to the yogi. Whatever man displays such great resolution will be successful.

The Baital[1] then said to the King, "Who are you and where are you taking me?"

He replied, "I am the King Vikram and I am taking you off to a yogi."

[1] Bytal, a kind of wraith like evil spirit, which is said to enter into and for a while re-animate dead bodies.

The Baital said, "I will go, on condition that I shall return if you speak on the road." The King agreed to this condition.

Upon this the Baital said, "King! Learned men; men of sense and intelligence pass their days in the delights of Shastras and of songs. Stupid persons and fools pass their time in ease and sleep. For this reason, it is better that we should beguile the road with profitable conversation; listen, while I tell you a story."

THE FIRST TALE

There was a Rajah of Benares, named Pratab Mukut, who had a son, named Bajra Mukut, whose wife's name was Mahadevi.

One day the young prince went out on an excursion, taking his minister's son with him. They advanced a great distance into the jungle; and in the middle saw a beautiful tank. On the edge were wild geese, Brahmini-ducks, male and female cranes and waterfowl. On all four sides, ghats of brick had been built; lotuses were in full bloom in the tank.

On the banks were trees of different kinds. In the shade the breeze was cool, and birds were singing in the branches. In the forest many coloured flowers blossomed, on which swarms of bees were buzzing.

They arrived at the bank of the tank and, after having washed their faces and hands, they fastened their horses. They went inside a temple and offered adoration to Mahadev.

Whilst they were in the temple, a certain princess, accompanied by a crowd of attendants, came to another bank of the tank to bathe. Having bathed and finished her meditations and prayers, she took her attendants with her and began to walk about under the shade of the trees.

The minister's son was sitting down. The prince was wandering about when suddenly his eyes met the princess' eyes. The prince was fascinated with her beauty, and began to say to himself, "O vile Cupid! Why do you vex me?"

The princess, when she saw the young prince, took in her hand the flower of the lotus. Having worshipped it, she put it to her head and, after putting it to her ear and biting it with her teeth, placed it under her feet. Again taking it up, she placed it in her bosom and accompanied by her attendants, mounted her conveyance and went home.

And the prince, greatly dispirited and drowned in sorrow, came to the minister's son. With a feeling of shame, he began to explain his state to him, "O friend, I have seen a most beautiful damsel, whose name and residence I do not know; if I do not obtain her, I will not live. I am resolutely determined in my mind."

When the minister's son heard these circumstances, he caused the prince to mount, and brought him home. The prince was so restless from grief at separation from the damsel, that he abandoned writing, reading, eating, drinking, sleep, the affairs of his government, and everything else. He constantly drew her picture, looked at it, and wept. He never spoke or listened to anyone else.

When the minister's son saw the state to which the young prince had been reduced, he said to him, "Whosoever enters on the path of love, cannot survive; and, if by chance he should live, he suffers great grief. For this reason, wise men avoid this path."

The prince, on hearing his remarks, replied, "I have entered on this path, whatever the result may be, whether pleasure or pain.

When he heard this determined speech, the minister's son said, "O great king! At the time of going away did she say anything to you, or did you say anything to her?"

He replied, "I neither said anything nor did I hear her say anything."

Then the minister's son said, "It will be difficult to find her."

The young prince replied, "If I obtain her, I shall live, otherwise my life is gone."

The minister's son again enquired, "Did she or not make any sign?"

The young prince replied, "This is what she did when she saw me; she took a lotus flower from her head and, after putting it to her ear bit it with her teeth, placed it under her feet and then put it in her bosom."

On hearing this, the minister's son said, "I understand her signs, and have found out her name and place of abode."

The prince replied, "If you understand the signs, explain them to me."

He began to say, "Prince! By taking the lotus from her head and putting it to her ear, she meant to explain to you that she was an inhabitant of the Carnatic[2]. And by putting it under her feet, she meant to say that her name was Padmawatti and by biting it with her teeth, she meant that she was the daughter of King Dantbat. And by taking it up again, and fastening it on her breast, she meant that you dwell in her bosom."

When the young prince had heard this much, he said, "It is advisable that you take me to the city in which she dwells." On his saying this they dressed and armed themselves. Taking some jewels with them, they mounted their horses and travelled to where she lived.

They soon arrived in the country of the Carnatic and, while wandering about the city; they came to the palace of the King. There was an old woman sitting at her door and plying her cotton wheel.

The two dismounted, approached her and said, "Mother! We are travelling merchants; our goods are coming after us. We have come in advance to search for a place to live in. If you will give us a place, we will live there."

The old woman, on looking at their faces and hearing what they asked, took compassion on them, and said, "This house is yours; remain here as long as you please."

So they went into the house and lived there; and after some delay, the old woman came and sat with them. The minister's son said to her, "Who are the members of your family and your relations, and how do you earn a subsistence?"

The old woman said, "My son is very well off and comfortable in the service of the King; and I am the wet nurse of Padmawatti, the King's daughter. Because of my advanced age I dwell in this house; but the King provides for my maintenance. I go once a day to see the damsel and then return to my own grief at home."

The prince, being glad to hear these words, said to the old woman, "When you go tomorrow to the maiden, please carry a message from me to her."

She replied, "Son! What need is there for putting it off until tomorrow? I will immediately convey your message."

He then said, "Go and say to her that the prince, whom she saw on the bank of the tank on the fifth day of the moon of the light part of the month Jeth, has arrived here."

On hearing these words, the old woman, taking a stick in her hand went to the royal palace and found the princess sitting there alone. When the old woman appeared before her, the prin-

[2] Pronounced by natives Karnatak.

cess made a salaam. The old woman, having given her a blessing, said, "Daughter! I attended and suckled you in your infancy. Bhagwan has now increased your stature. My heart desires to see the happiness of your youth, in order that I also may be at ease."

Having talked in this affectionate manner, she began to say, "The prince, whom you met on the fifth day of the moon in the light part of the month Jeth, on the bank of a tank, has come to my house. He has sent you this message. And I also tell you, that the Prince is worthy of you, and is as excellent in disposition and mental qualities as you are beautiful."

When the maiden heard all these speeches she was angry; and taking a sandal in her hands, slapped the cheeks of the old woman, saying, "Unfortunate creature! Get out of my house." The old woman was distressed at this command and rose up immediately and returned to the young prince, mentioning all that had occurred.

The prince was aghast at hearing these words. Upon this, the minister's son said, "O great king! Be not at all anxious; you have not understood what has happened."

He replied, "What you say is true, but explain the circumstances to me, so that my mind may be at rest."

He said, "By putting a sandal on her ten fingers and striking the old woman in the face she meant that, when the remaining ten nights of moonlight have passed, she will meet you in the dark."

After ten days the old woman went again, and spoke about the young prince. The princess covered three of her fingers with saffron and struck the old woman on the neck, and said, "Get out of my house."

At length the old woman went away quite in despair. She came and informed the Prince of what had happened. On hearing her statement, he was drowned in a river of sorrow.

Seeing him in this state, the minister's son said, "Suffer not anxiety; the meaning of this circumstance is somewhat different."

The young prince replied, "My mind is disquieted; tell me quickly the meaning."

The minister's son said, "She is menstruating and has therefore made a further delay of three days; she will send for you on the fourth day."

When the three days had elapsed, the old woman made inquiries after the health of the princess on the part of the young prince. The maiden was angry, and brought the old woman to the western door of the house, and turned her out. When the old woman came and mentioned these circumstances to the prince, he became sad at hearing the account.

In the meanwhile the minister's son said, "The explanation of the case is this, that she has invited you to meet this night by the door."

The prince was highly delighted at hearing this; when the time came, they dressed themselves in purple suits, and wore gracefully arranged turbans, and armed themselves with weapons of all kinds. After midnight when there was profound silence they went along quietly, and without noise of any kind, arrived at the door. The minister's son stayed outside, and the young prince went in.

As he entered he saw the princess standing there, awaiting his arrival. Their eyes met and the princess laughed; and, having shut the door, took the young prince with her to an apartment dedicated to voluptuous enjoyment. There he saw censers in which perfumes were burnt. Female attendants wearing dresses of various colours were standing respectfully, each according to her rank, with her hands folded.

On one side, a bed of flowers was spread, with pawn-boxes, rose water bottles, trays and boxes with four partitions. On the other side, compound essences, prepared sandalwood, mixed perfumes, musk, and saffron were deposited in metal cups. Here and there were coloured boxes scattered about containing well-prepared confections, and there were sweetmeats of different kinds. All the doors and walls were adorned with drawings and pictures and in them were such enchanting figures. In short, everything was provided that could contribute to pleasure. The whole scene was so extraordinary as to baffle description.

The princess Padmawatti took the young prince to an apartment and offered him a seat. She washed his feet and had sandalwood rubbed upon his body. Garlands of flowers were fastened upon his neck and rose water was sprinkled over him. She began to fan him with her own hands.

Upon this the prince said, "Why do you take so much trouble? By seeing you I have become cool. Those delicate hands of yours are not adapted for plying the fan. Give it to me, and you sit down."

Padmawatti said, "O great king! You have gone to great trouble to come here for my sake; it is only right that I should wait upon you."

Then an attendant, having taken the fan from the princess' hands said, "This is my business; I will attend upon you and you both enjoy yourselves."

Then they began to eat and to carry on a friendly conversation. Meanwhile the day dawned, the princess kept him concealed, and, when it was night, they engaged in amorous pleasures. In this way several days passed. When the prince wished to depart, the princess would not let him go.

A month was thus spent and the prince was greatly perplexed and very anxious. One night he was sitting alone and thinking to himself, "I have given up my country, government, throne, family and everything else. For a month I have not once met with the friend through whom I obtained this happiness. What will he say, and how do I know what may have happened to him?"

He was sitting occupied with such anxious thoughts when the princess came to the spot and, seeing the state he was in, began to enquire, "O great king! Tell me what grief you suffer which makes you sit down so sad?"

He said, "I have a very dear friend, the son of the minister, and, for a month past I have not heard anything of him. He is such an intelligent and learned friend, that through his merit and skill I have met you, and he explained all your secrets to me."

The princess said, "O great king! Your soul is there, how will you be able to enjoy happiness here? It is better that I should prepare some sweetmeats and have them sent there so that you can go there yourself. Having entertained him and given him great consolation, you can return with your mind at ease."

On hearing this, the prince rose up and the princess had sweetmeats of different kinds with poison mixed in them prepared. The prince had gone to the minister's son, and was sitting with him, when the sweetmeats arrived.

The minister's son enquired, "O great king! How did these sweetmeats come here?"

The prince replied, "I was sitting at the princess' house, sad at the thought of you, when she came and enquired why I was in low spirits. When she heard the circumstances, she gave me permission to come to you and has had these sweetmeats sent in order that you also may be gratified."

The minister's son said, "You have brought poison for me; it is just as well you have not eaten it yourself. O great king! Listen to one remark from me—A woman never loves her lover's friend, you have not done well in mentioning my name to her."

On hearing this, the prince replied, "No one ever would do this. If a mortal feared not his fellow mortal, he would have a dread of God." With these words he threw one of the sweetmeats to a dog, which fell down dead in convulsions as soon as he had eaten it.

The prince was enraged, and began to say, "It is not proper to associate with such a woman; hitherto I had an affection for her, but now I have found her out."

When the minister's son heard these words, he said, "O great king! What has happened has happened; you must now adopt measures to take her to your house."

The prince replied, "Brother! This too must be done by you."

The minister's son replied, "Today do this one thing, go again to Padmawatti and do what I tell you. When you first approach her, show great love and fondness for her; and when she goes to sleep, take off her jewels, and strike her on the left thigh with this trident."

Having heard this, the prince went to Padmawatti at night. After a long and affectionate conversation, they slept together, but the prince was secretly watching for his opportunity. At length, when the princess was asleep, he took off all her ornaments, and having struck her on the left thigh with the trident, came to his own house. Having explained all the circumstances to the minister's son, he put down all the ornaments before him. He now assumed the appearance of a yogi, and taking the prince with him, went and sat down in a place where bodies are burnt.

He became a spiritual preceptor, and making the prince his pupil, said to him, "Go into the bazaar and sell these jewels. If anyone shall lay hold of you while you are thus engaged, bring him to me."

Having heard what he said the prince went with the jewels to the city and showed them to a jeweller. On seeing them he recognised them, and said, "These jewels belong to the King's daughter; say truly where you got them."

While he was talking to the prince, ten or twenty other persons collected together on the spot. At length the prince was apprehended and asked to state truly where he had got them.

The prince said that his spiritual preceptor had given them to him to sell but he did not know how he had obtained possession of them.

The spiritual preceptor was also apprehended and brought to the King's presence. When the King had heard the case, he began to enquire from the yogi, "Master! Where did you obtain possession of these ornaments?"

The devotee said, "O great king! On the fourteenth of the dark lunar fortnight, I went to a place were dead bodies are burnt, for the purpose of having a witch's incantation accomplished. When the witch came, I took off her ornaments and clothes, and made a mark with a trident on her thigh. In this way the ornaments came into my possession."

Having heard the yogi's statement, the King went into the female apartments, and the yogi sat down upon his asun[3].

The King said to the queen, "See if there is a mark on Padmawatti's left thigh, and what sort of mark it is."

The queen went and saw there was the mark of a trident, and when she came back, she said to the King, "O great king! There are three even marks, as though someone had struck her with a trident."

When the King had heard this account he said, "Go and bring the yogi here."

The King, reflecting in his mind, began to say, "It is not proper to reveal to anyone our family affairs and the designs of our hearts, and our losses."

In the meanwhile the yogi came and the King, having taken him aside enquired, "Gosain Ji! What punishment is written in the Dharma Shastra for a woman?"

The yogi replied, "O great king! If a Brahmin, a cow, a wife, a child or any other person shall be guilty of a perfidious act, it is written that the person should be banished from the country."

Having heard this, the King had Padmawatti conveyed away in a doli and abandoned in a jungle. The prince and the minister's son both mounted their horses and, having left Padmawatti in the jungle, they continued to their city.

After some days both arrived at their houses. All persons, whether of high or low degree, were highly delighted and happy."

Having related so much of the story, the Baital asked King Vir Vikramaditya, "Who was at fault of those four? If you do not explain this you will fall into the infernal regions."

[3] Asan—Lit. A seat—which religious mendicants generally carry with them, some a deer skin, others a leopard or tiger skin, and on which they usually sit. The hide of a black male antelope is a favourite asan; some of the Hindu Gods are fabled to use the lotus flower for this purpose.

King Vikramaditya said, "The King is at fault?"

The Baital replied, "The minister's son performed his master's business and the daughter accomplished what she desired, therefore the King was to blame for having banished her without due consideration."

On hearing these words he returned to that place and having climbed the tree fastened the corpse, and placing it upon his shoulder, took it away with him.

Then the Baitạl said, "King! The second story is as follows."

THE SECOND TALE

On the bank of the Jamuna, there is a city named Dharamasthal, the King of which is named Gunadhip. There is a Brahmin there, whose name is Keshav, who constantly repeats prayers and performs acts of penance on the banks of the Jamuna; his daughter's name was Madhumawatti and she was very beautiful.

When she was of a fit age to be married, her mother, father and brother considered her possible marriage. It so happened that her father went to a customer's marriage, and her brother to the house of a spiritual preceptor in the village. After they had both gone, a Brahmin's son came to the house. Her mother, having seen his excellent qualities and personal beauty, said to him; "I will marry my daughter to you." However the Brahmin meanwhile had consented at his customer's house to give his daughter in marriage to a Brahmin's son; and the Brahmin's son had promised a Brahmin at the place where he had gone to read, to give him his sister.

After some days, the father and son, came home with the two young Brahmins, and before their arrival, the third was already sitting in the house. One was named Tribikram, the second Baman, and the third Madhusudan; they were all equal in good looks, mental qualities and age. The Brahmin, when he saw them, began to reflect; "There is one virgin, and there are three bridegrooms; to whom shall I give her? We three are under promises to these three; this is a strange business. What can be done?"

He was sitting occupied with these thoughts when a snake bit the girl, and she died. When they heard of this, all five ran off and brought back with them all the exorcists and persons skilled in charms and incantations against poisons they could find. On seeing the girl, all said that she could not be restored to life.

The first said, "A person does not survive, who has been bitten by a snake on the fifth, sixth, eighth, ninth, or fourteenth day of the lunar month."

The second said, "A person also bitten on a Saturday or Tuesday will not live."

The third said, "Poison infused during the Rohini, Magha, Ashlekha, Vishaka, Mul, and Kritika mansions of the moon, does not come out."

The fourth said, "A person bitten in the organs of sense, in the lips, cheeks, neck, abdomen, navel, in any of these parts, cannot escape death."

The fifth said, "In this case, Bramha himself could not restore her to life; of what avail are we? You should now perform her funeral obsequies, and we will take our leave."

Having thus spoken, the men skilled in charms and incantations went away; and the Brahmin took the corpse and had it burnt at the usual place.

After this the three young men did as follows: — One of them, selecting and fastening together some of the burnt bones, became a fakir and wandered through different forests. The second tied her ashes in a bundle, built a small hut there and began to live on the spot where her corpse was burnt. The third became a yogi and, taking her wallet and necklace, began to travel from country to country. One day he went to a Brahmin's house. The Brahmin began to say, "Be so good as to eat your food here today."

At these words he sat down. The Brahmin had his guest's feet and hands washed and took him to where the food was prepared. His wife had come to serve out the food when her youngest son came, crying and grabbed hold of his mother's dress. She tried to make him let go, but he would not; and the more she coaxed him, the more he cried, and the more obstinate he became. Upon this the Brahmin's wife, being angry, took the child and threw him into the fire; the child was burnt to ashes.

When the Brahmin saw this done, he rose up without eating anything. Then the man of the house said, "Why do you not eat?"

He replied, "How can anyone eat food in a house in which a diabolical act has been committed?"

Having heard these words the householder rose up, and went to bring a book on the science of restoring life. Extracting a charm from it, he repeated prayers to restore his son to life. When the Brahmin saw this wonderful act performed, he began to reflect, "If

I could obtain possession of the book, I too could restore my beloved to life."

Having resolved to obtain possession of it, he ate his food, and remained there.

Late at night all had eaten supper and gone to sleep. The Brahmin had also gone to bed, but remained awake. When he thought that all in the house were asleep, he took the book and went away with it. After some days, he came to the place where he had burnt the Brahmin's daughter's body. He found the other two Brahmins there, sat down and entered into conversation.

The two Brahmins said, "Brother! You have wandered from country to country, but tell us have you learnt any science?" He said, "I have learnt the science of restoring the dead to life."

They replied, "If you have learnt the science, restore our beloved to life."

He said, "Make a heap of the ashes and bones and I will restore her to life."

They collected the ashes and bones together, and having taken a charm from the book, he repeated some prayers, and the girl rose up restored to life. Then Cupid so blinded them that they began to wrangle with each other."

Having related so much of the story, the Baital said, "King! Explain whose wife she should be?"

King Vikram said, "She belonged to him who built the yogi's hut and dwelt there."

The Baital said, "If one of them had not kept her bones, how could she have lived; and if the second Brahmin had not learnt the science of vivifying, how could he have restored her to life?"

The King replied, "He who kept her bones occupied the place of her son, and he who restored her to life was, as it were, her father. She therefore became the wife of him who kept her ashes and dwelt in a hut at the place where her body had been burnt."

Having heard this answer, the Baital climbed up the tree again, and became suspended; and the King, having followed and found him, placed him upon his shoulder, and carried him off again.

THE THIRD TALE

The Baital said, "King! There is a city named Bardwan, in which there was a King whose name was Rupsen. It happened one day that the King was sitting in a house near his own gate, when he heard the sound of some people outside.

The King said, "Who is at the door, and what noise is it I hear?"

The doorkeeper replied, "O great king! You have asked a very proper question; many persons come and sit at the threshold of a sick man's house for the purpose of taking away his life and property."

When the King heard this, he remained silent. In the meantime a traveller named Birbar, a Rajput, came to the King's door, in the hope of obtaining service. The doorkeeper, having ascertained his circumstances, said to the King, "O great king! An armed man has come in the expectation of employment and if he obtains your Highness's permission, he will come into your presence." Having heard this the King gave the order to bring him and the doorkeeper went and brought him.

Upon this the King enquired, "Oh Rajput! What shall I give you for your daily expenses?"

Birbur having heard this said, "Give me a thousand tolahs of gold daily, and I shall be able to subsist."

The Rajah enquired, "How many people are there with you?"

He said, "First my wife; second, my son; third, my daughter; fourth, myself."

When they heard him speak thus, all the people of the King's court turned aside and began to laugh. The King began to consider why the Rajput had asked for so much money. He thought to himself that if he gave him a great deal, it might turn to an advantage someday. With this idea in his mind, he sent for his treasurer, and said, "Give daily from my treasury a thousand tolahs of gold to this Birbar."

Having heard this command, Birbar took a thousand tolahs of gold for that day and divided it into shares. He distributed half of it to the Brahmins and, having divided the remaining half into two portions, gave one portion to the pilgrims, byragees and the worshippers of Vishnu, sanyasis. With the remaining portion he prepared food and fed the poor; the remainder he kept for his own use.

In this manner he constantly subsisted with his wife and children. Each day in the evening he went to guard the King's bed with his shield and sword. Whenever the King awoke from sleep and called out, "Is anyone present?" the Rajput replied, "Birbar is present; whatever order you give he will obey."

He thus remained vigilant all night; moreover, whether he was eating, drinking, asleep, moving or wandering about, he continued to be mindful of his master.

Now it is happened one night that the sound of a woman crying came from a place where the bodies of the dead were burnt. The King, having heard the noise, called out, "Is anyone present?" Birbur, on hearing these words, said, "I am present and ready to execute any order."

The King ordered him to go to the spot where the sound of the crying came from, to find out the reason for her weeping. When the Rajput received the order, he went to the place where the woman was crying. The King, unknown to Birbar, followed him, dressed in black, to test his courage.

In the meanwhile Birbar arrived at the place where bodies were burnt, and where the woman was crying. There he saw a beautiful female loaded with jewels from head to foot and lamenting bitterly. Sometimes she danced, sometimes she wept, and sometimes she ran about. There was not a tear in her eyes; but beating her head, and uttering cries of lamentation, she dashed herself on the ground.

Observing these circumstances, Birbar enquired from her, "Why are you crying and beating yourself so violently? Who are you and what grief afflicts you?"

She replied, "I am the good genie of the King."

Birbar said, "What is the reason for your weeping?"

She then began to explain to Birbar, "Soon in the King's house, poverty will come to his family, and I shall leave him. After the lapse of a month the King will die, having endured great affliction; this is why I am weeping. I have caused great happiness in his family and therefore what must happen is to me a subject of regret. What I now say cannot in any way prove to be untrue."

Birbar then enquired, "Is there anyway in which the King may escape and live for a hundred years?"

She said, "In the eastern quarter is a temple of Devi; if you will present your son's head to the Devi, having cut it off with your own hand, the King will reign a hundred years without any interruption."

On hearing these words Birbar went home, and the King also followed. When he reached home, having awakened his wife, he explained everything that had happened to him in detail.

When she heard this she awakened her son, "Son! By offering your head the King's life will be saved."

Having heard this the boy said, "Mother! Firstly, I am bound to respect your order; secondly I am bound to promote my master's wishes; thirdly, if this body can be of use to a divinity, there is nothing better in the world. In my opinion, it is not right to delay in this matter."

Birbar said, "If you will give up your child willingly, I will take him away, and offer him as sacrifice for the King's sake."

She replied, "Son, daughter, brother, relations, mother, father, and all others are nothing to me; I look to you alone."

Her son said, "Father! Whoever can advance his master's interests in the world may live to good purpose, and is benefited in both worlds by doing so." Her daughter then said, "If a mother gives poison to her daughter, and a father sells his son, and a King takes everything away from a subject, to whom can these look for protection?"

The four, reflecting and conversing thus with each other, went to the temple of Devi; the King went also after them secretly. Birbar arrived at the temple and performed adoration to Devi. He began to say with joined hands, "O Devi! Grant that by sacrificing my son, the King may live for a hundred years!"

Having thus spoken, he cut off his son's head, which fell to the ground. On seeing her brother's death, the daughter inflicted a wound on her neck with a sword, by which her head was separated from her body. When she saw the death of her son and daughter,

Birbar's wife gave herself such a wound on the back of the neck that her head was also severed from her body. Having seen the death of these three, Birbar, reflecting, began to say, "Since my family is dead, for whom shall I continue to perform service?" Having thus considered, he struck himself such a blow with a sword on the back of his neck, that his head was separated from his body. And on seeing the death of those four persons, the King said to himself, "The lives of Birbar's family have been sacrificed for my sake; it would be an accursed thing to carry on government now." With these thoughts in his mind, the King was on the point of killing himself with his sword, when the Devi came and laid hold of his hand, and said, "Son! I have been delighted with your resolution, I will grant you whatever boon you may ask me."

The King replied, "Mother! If you have been delighted, restore these four persons to life."

Devi said, "This shall be," and on saying these words, having brought the water of immortality, she restored the four to life. After this the King divided his kingdom with Birbar."

Having related this much, the Baital said, "How happy is that servant, who did not hesitate to sacrifice his own life and the lives of his family for the sake of his master. How happy is the King who did not exhibit a longing greedy desire, either for his government or his life! Oh King! I ask you this question, whose virtue was the greatest?"

King Vikramaditya said, "The King's virtue was the greatest."

The Baital enquired, "Why?"

The King answered, "It is becoming in a servant to give his life for his master, but the King abandoned his government and throne, and did not value his life a straw for his sake, and therefore, the King's virtue exceeded that of the others."

Having heard this words, the Baital went again, and was suspended on the tree, in the place where the bodies of the dead were burnt; and the King, having gone there, bound him and took him away.

THE FOURTH TALE

Then the Baital said, "King! There is a city named Bhagwatti, the King of which is Rupsen, who has a parrot called Churaman.

One day the King enquired from the parrot, "What do you know?"

The parrot said, "O great king! I know everything."

The King said, "If you have knowledge of the subject, explain where there is an elegant damsel equal in rank to me."

Then the parrot replied, "O great king! In the Magadh country, there is a King named Magadheswar, and his daughter's name is Chandrawatti; you shall be married to her, as she is very beautiful and learned."

The King, having heard this speech from the parrot, sent for an astrologer named Chandrakant and enquired, "To which damsel shall I be married?"

Having ascertained it by means of astrology, he said, "There is a virgin named Chandrawatti to whom you shall be married."

The King, having heard these words, called a Brahmin and, explaining everything to him, said, as he sent him to the King Magadheswar, "If you arrange successfully for my marriage, I will make you happy."

Having heard these words, the Brahmin took leave. The King of Magadheswar's daughter had a mynah bird, named Madanmanjari. The King's daughter one day enquired from Madanmanjari, "Where is there a husband worthy of me?"

The mynah replied, "King Rupsen of the city Bhagwatti shall be your husband."

In short, without seeing one another, each had become enamoured of the other. Now the Brahmin also came there and delivered the message of his own King to the King Magadheswar, who agreed to what the Brahmin proposed. "Send the nuptial gifts and all customary things. Go and present my respects to the King and, having made the customary marks on his forehead, return quickly; when you come back, I will make preparations for the marriage."

These two Brahmins started thence and after some days arrived at the abode of King Rupsen, and mentioned all that had taken place at the other King's. The King was pleased so the arrangements were made for the marriage. When the marriage ceremony was over, he took the bridal gifts and dowry and went to his own kingdom. The King's daughter also, at the time of setting out, took Madanmanjari's cage with her, and after some days they arrived in their palace.

It happened one day that both the cages of the parrot and the mynah had been placed near the throne. The King and Queen began to say to each other, "No-one can pass life in solitude; it is better to marry the mynah and parrot together, and place them in one cage, that they may live happily."

So a large cage was brought and both placed in it. After some days, the King and Queen were sitting conversing with each other, when the parrot began to say to the mynah, "In this world sexual connection is the root of every living thing. Those who have not had sexual connection have passed away to no purpose; for this reason let me have sexual connection with you."

Having heard this the mynah said, "I have no desire for connection with a male."

The parrot asked, "Why?" and the mynah said, "Men are sinful and devoid of religion, treacherous, and murderers of women."

The parrot, having heard this, said, "Women are also deceitful, false, ignorant, avaricious, and murderers."

When they both began to argue, the King enquired, "Why are you arguing with each other?"

The mynah said, "O great king! Men are sinners and murderers of women, and therefore I have no desire for a male. O great king! Please listen while I mention one thing to prove that men are such."

THE STORY OF THE MYNAH BIRD

There was a city named Ilapur, in which was a very wealthy merchant who had no family. For this reason he was constantly performing pilgrimages, fasting and listening continually to the Puranas, and bestowing many gifts upon Brahmins. After some time, by the pleasure of God, a son was born to the merchant. He celebrated the birth with great splendour and bestowed many presents upon Brahmins and bards; and gave to the hungry, the thirsty, and the poor.

When the son was five years old he was taught to read; he used to go from his father's house to read, but on arrival amongst the other boys used to gamble with them.

After sometime the merchant died, and his son having become master, spent his days in gambling, and his nights in fornication. Having thus dissipated all his wealth in a few years he quitted his country, utterly ruined. Later he arrived at the city of Chandrapur, where a very rich merchant, named Hemgupta lived. He went to him and mentioned the name and circumstances of his father.

He was pleased at hearing them and embraced him, and enquired the reason of his coming. He replied, "I had taken a ship and gone to an island for the purpose of trading. Having gone there and sold all my goods and taken other articles on board, I started in the ship for my own country. Suddenly such a storm arose, that the ship was wrecked, and I was left sitting on a plank, and I have came here floating on it. Now I am ashamed at having lost all my property and wealth, and how can I in this condition go and show my face to the inhabitants of my own city?"

When he had spoken thus in the presence of the merchant, the merchant began to reflect, "God has offered an opportunity, it is not right to delay. The best plan is to marry my daughter to him; whatever can be done now is best; who knows what will happen tomorrow?"

Having formed this idea in his mind, he came to his wife and said to her, "A merchant's son has come; if you consent we will marry our daughter Rattanawatti to him."

She was pleased at hearing the proposal, and said, "Sah Jee! Such a union is only formed by the intervention of God himself, because the desires of our minds have been accomplished while we were sitting quietly at home. For this reason, it is better not to delay."

The merchant having then summoned a Brahmin, fixed an auspicious time and gave his daughter in marriage, bestowing a large dowry upon her.

At length, when the marriage had been formalised, they began to live together at the merchant's house. After some days the bridegroom said to the merchant's daughter, "My mind is sad at the thought that it is a long time since I came into your country and I have not received any news of my own home and family. I have explained all my circumstances to you; you ought now to persuade your mother to allow me to take leave and go to my own city, and you should come also."

So she said to her mother, "My husband wishes to go to his country; please act now, so that his mind may not be upset."

The merchant's wife went to her husband and said, "Your son-in-law has asked for permission to go to his own home."

Having heard this the merchant said, "Well, we will let him go, because we have no power over another person's son; we will act so as to please him."

Having spoken thus, he called his daughter and said to her, "Tell me, will you go to your father-in-law's family, or remain in your mother's house?"

The daughter was ashamed and gave no answer, and returned to her husband and said to him, "My father and mother have said that they will act so as to please you; do not leave us."

At length the merchant having sent for his son-in-law and bestowed great wealth upon him allowed him and his daughter to depart with a doli (palanquin) and a female servant.

On their way, they arrived at a jungle, and he said to the merchant's daughter, "There is great danger here. Give me the jewels, I will fasten them round my waist and when you come to the outskirts of the city, you can wear them again."

On hearing this, she took off all her ornaments. He took them and dismissed the bearers, and then he killed the female servant. Then he threw her body into a well and pushed his wife down another well. Taking all the ornaments, he went off to his own country.

In the meantime, a traveller came along the road, and having heard the sound of weeping, stopped and began to say, "From where does the sound of mortal weeping come in this jungle?"

Having thus reflected, he went to the well. On peering over, he saw a woman in tears. "Who are you, and how did you fall into this well?" he said.

She said, "I am the daughter of the merchant Hemgupta and was travelling with my husband to his own country, when thieves came and surrounded us. Having killed my female servant, they threw me into a well, and bound my husband then carried him off together with my jewels. I have no news of him, nor he of me."

Having heard this, the traveller escorted her to the merchant's door. She went to her mother and father, who enquired, "What has happened to you?"

She said, "Thieves came and robbed me on the road, and, having killed my female servant and thrown her into a well, pushed me into another well. Then, having bound my husband, they carried him off together with my ornaments. When they began to ask for more money, I said, "You have taken all I had, what have I left now? Now I don't know whether they put him to death or let him go."

Upon this her father said, "Daughter! Be not anxious, your husband is alive, and, by the will of God, will be restored to you in a few days, because thieves seek money and not life."

The merchant presented her with other ornaments in exchange for those she had lost, and gave her great comfort and consolation. And the merchant's son-in-law, having arrived at his home and sold all the ornaments, began to pass his days and nights in debauchery with women. He began to gamble to such an extent that all his money was lost and he was again in want of food.

At last, when he began to suffer very great distress, he thought that he would go to his father-in-law's house, and pretend that a grandson had been born, and that he had come to congratulate him on the event. Having resolved upon this, he started on his journey and arrived there after some days. When he was about to enter the merchant's house, his wife saw her husband was coming, and said to herself, "May he not turn back from fear."

In the meantime she approached him and said, "Husband! Do not worry, I have told my father that thieves came and killed my female servant, and having made me take off all my ornaments and thrown me into a well, they bound you and carried you off. You also tell the same story. Be not at all anxious; the house is yours."

Having thus spoken she went into the house and he went to the merchant, who rose up and embraced him and enquired into his story. He told everything just as his wife had instructed him to do. There was rejoicing throughout the house. After this, the merchant placed food before him and treating him with great favour, said, "This house is yours, live happily here."

He remained there and, after some days, the merchant's daughter came to sleep with him, wearing her jewels, and fell asleep. At midnight, when he saw that she was fast asleep, he cut her throat with a knife so that she died. Having stripped her of all her ornaments, he went off to his own country.

Having narrated this much, the mynah said, "O great king! This, I have seen with my own eyes, and, therefore, have no desire for a man. The disposition of man is so like that of a highway robber who could form a friendship with such a being and nourish a snake in his bosom? O great king! Be pleased to consider, what crime had the woman committed?"

Having heard this, the King said, "Oh parrot! Tell me what faults there are in woman." Then the parrot said, "O great king! Please listen."

STORY OF THE PARROT

There is a city named Kanchanpur, in which a merchant, named Sagardutt, had a son whose name was Shridutt. There was another city named Sherijpur, in which was a merchant, named Somdutt, whose daughter's named was Jayshri. She was married to Shridutt, and as he had gone abroad trading, she used to stay with her mother and father.

When he had spent twelve years in trading, and the young girl had grown up, she began to say one day to a female companion, "Sister! My youth is thus passing away, I have not experienced any of the pleasures of the world."

Having heard this, her companion replied, "Be of good cheer, God willing, your husband will quickly come to you."

On hearing this she was angry and, ascending a balcony, peeped through a lattice and saw a young man coming along. When he came nearer their eyes met and the hearts of both were affected with the passion of love. She then said to her companion, "Bring that person to me."

Having heard this, the companion went and said to him, "Somdutt's daughter has sent for you in private, come to my house; and she pointed out to him where her house was.

He replied, "I will come at night." The companion came and told the merchant's daughter that he had said he would come at night.

Having heard this, Jayshri said to her companion, "Go to your house inform me when he comes, and I will also come at my leisure."

The companion began to watch for him. When he came she said, "Sit here," and she came and said to Jayshri, "Your beloved has come."

On hearing this she said, "Wait a little, I will come when the people of the house are asleep."

When it was midnight and all were asleep, she rose up silently and went with her companion to the house. Instantly both met without restraint and, when four ghurees of the night remained, she rose and went quietly to her own house, where she fell asleep. He also went home at dawn.

Many days were spent thus. At length her husband came from a foreign country to his father-in-law's house. When she saw her husband, she reflected in her own mind and said to her companion, "Such is my anxiety; what shall I do, whither shall I go? I have forgotten sleep, hunger, and thirst; I have neither pleasure in standing nor in sitting," and she explained all her thoughts to her.

In the evening, when her husband had eaten, his mother-in-law sent him a message to go and sleep in the pavilion, and she told her daughter to go and wait upon him.

On hearing this, she turned up her nose, pouted and remained silent. Her mother threatened her and told her to go again. She, having no alternative, went there and reclined on the bed with her face averted. He spoke affectionately to her, and the more he did so, the more vexed she was. He also gave her dresses and jewels of different kinds, which he had brought for her from every country, and said, "Wear these."

She then became still more angry and raising her eyebrows, turned her face. In despair, he went to sleep because he was fatigued with his journey. But she could not sleep. When she knew that her husband was fast asleep, she rose up softly and, having left him asleep went fearlessly in the dark night to the lover's house.

A thief, having seen her on the road, thought to himself "Where is this woman going alone at midnight with jewels on?" Having thus said to himself, he followed her. Somehow or other she arrived at her lover's house. A snake had bitten him and he was dead.

She thought he was lying asleep; and burning with the fire of separation she embraced him with the utmost affection. The thief beheld this sight from a distance.

An evil spirit was sitting on a peepal tree there and looking on. It suddenly occurred to him to enter into the corpse and thus have sexual connection with her. Having come into the body, the evil spirit had connection with her, and afterwards bit off her nose with his teeth.

The thief saw all the circumstances and she, in despair and covered with blood, went to her companion and told her all that had happened.

Her companion said, "Go quickly to your husband before the sun has risen. Having gone there, weep most violently; if anyone asks you the reason for your weeping, say that he has cut off your nose."

On hearing the advice of her companion, she went off instantly, and began to weep immoderately. On hearing the sound of her crying, all her relations came, and saw that she had no nose. Then they said to her husband, "O shameless, criminal compassionless, ignorant wretch! Why have you cut off her nose when she has done nothing wrong?"

She too, on seeing this farce going on, began to say to herself. "Everyone should be afraid of the acts of a woman, what power have men of knowing them?"

In the meantime the police came and, having bound the husband, brought him to the kotwal. The kotwal informed the King who, having sent for the husband, asked him what had happened; and he replied "that he knew nothing about it."

And when he had sent for the merchant's daughter and asked her, she said, "Having seen the outrage, that has been done me, why do you ask?"

The King said to the husband, "What punishment shall I inflict on you?"

He replied, "Whatever punishment you may determine to inflict"

The King said, "Take him away, and impale him."

The attendants having heard the King's order, took him away to impale him. The thief, who was looking on, and had seen all, that occurred, then raised a cry for justice. The King, having called him, enquired, "Who are you?"

He said, "Oh great king! I am a thief, and this man is guiltless, he is about to be murdered unjustly; you have not done justice."

Then the King caused the husband to be sent for, and said to the thief, "Say truly according to your religion, how has this affair happened?"

The thief explained all the circumstances in detail, and the King understood them well. At length messengers had the nose brought which had fallen into the mouth of the woman's lover who had fallen dead. Having seen it he knew that the husband was without fault, and that the thief had spoken truly.

Again the thief said, "O great king! It is excellence to cherish the good and punish the wicked."

The King, having caused the woman's face to be blackened, and her head to be shaved, had her carried round the city and let loose. Having given a pardon to the thief and merchant's son, he allowed them to take leave.

Having said this much, the parrot Churaman said, "O great king! Of such excellencies are all women composed!"

Having related this much, Baital said, "O King, who was the greater criminal of these two?"

Then the King Vir Vikramaditya said, "The woman."

Baital replied, "How so?"

The King said, "However depraved a man may be, he has some thought regarding right and wrong, but this woman had no such thought; therefore the woman was more criminal."

Having heard this, the Baital departed, and was suspended on the tree. The King, having gone again, took him down from the tree, and fastening him in a bundle, placed him on his shoulder and took him off.

THE FIFTH TALE

The Baital said, "There is a city named Ujjain, the King of which was named Mahabal, and his ambassador Haridas. The ambassador's daughter was Mahadevi, who was exceedingly beautiful.

When she was fit to be married, her father began to think on the subject and to seek for a bridegroom, fit to give his daughter to in marriage.

At length one day the daughter said to the father, "Father! Be pleased to marry me to a man possessed of universal skill and excellence."

He replied, "I will give you in marriage to someone who is acquainted with every science."

On another day the King, having called Haridas, said to him, "In the southern quarter there is a King, named Harichand; go to him and make enquiries for me regarding his health and welfare, and bring me information regarding them."

Having received the King's order, the ambassador took leave, and, after some days, arrived at the King Harichand's and delivered to him the message of his own King. He began to live constantly near the King.

It happened one day that the King asked him, "Haridas! Has the black age commenced or not?"

Then he, having joined his hands said, "The black age is present, O great king! Because there is great falsehood in the world, and the truth has been diminished. People talk smoothly with their mouths, and establish deceit in their hearts; religion is destroyed, crime has increased, and the earth has begun to give little fruit.

Kings have begun to levy fines; Brahmins have become avaricious; women have abandoned modesty; the son obeys not the orders of his father. The brother trusts not brother; friendship has departed from amongst friends; sincerity has left masters, servants have given up serving, and every kind of impropriety has made its appearance."

When he had thus spoken to the King, the King rose up and went into the female apartments; and the ambassador went and sat down in his own house.

In the meanwhile a Brahmin's son came to him and said, "I have come to ask something from you."

Having heard this, he said, "What request do you wish to make?"

He replied, "Give me your daughter in marriage."

Haridas said, "I will give her to a man, in whom excellent qualities shall be found."

The Brahmin's son said, "I understand all science."

He then said, "Show me some of your science, that I may know you understand it."

Then the Brahmin's son said, "I have made a four-wheeled carriage which will convey you in a second to wherever you want to go."

Haridas replied, "Please bring the four-wheeled carriage to me early in the morning."

He took the carriage to Haridas at dawn and they both mounted it and came to the city of Ujjain. Before his arrival, another Brahmin's son had come by and said to the ambassador's eldest son, "give me your sister in marriage." He also had replied, "I will give her to a man who understands all science," and that Brahmin's son had said that he understood all knowledge and science.

Having this heard this, he had said, "I will give her to you."

Another Brahmin's son had asked for the girl in marriage from her mother and she had also given this answer, "I will give my daughter to a man who understands all science.

That Brahmin's son had also said that he understood the science contained in all the Shastras; and that he could discharge an arrow, which should hit what, was merely heard and not seen.

When the mother had heard this, she consented to give her daughter to him.

In this manner the three bridegrooms were brought together. Haridas began to reflect in his mind, "There is one damsel and there are three bridegrooms; to whom shall I give her? He was occupied with this thought, when at night a demon came and carried her off to the top of the Vindhyachal mountains. It is said, "That excess of anything is not good. Sita was exceedingly beautiful and Ravana carried her off. King Bali bestowed many presents and became poor. Ravana ushered destruction on his family by indulging in excessive pride."

At length, when people did not see the young girl, they began to indulge in all kinds of conjectures. The three bridegrooms, having heard of the circumstances of her disappearance, came there also; Huridas asked the most intelligent of the three to explain where the young girl had gone.

After about a quarter of an hour's consideration one said, "A demon has carried off and deposited your daughter on a mountain." Upon this the second said "I will destroy the demon and bring her here," and the third said, "Mount my carriage and I will bring her here in it." On hearing these words, he mounted the carriage quickly, arrived at the mountain and killed the demon, and immediately brought the damsel back; and the three began to dispute amongst themselves.

Then the girl's father having reflected, said, "All three have acted with kindness, to whom shall I give her?" "

Having related so much of the tale, the Baital said "King Vikram! Whose wife did the young maiden become?"

The King said, "She became the wife of him who slew the demon, and brought her back."

The Baital said, "The virtues of all three were equal, how did she become the wife of him who slew the demon?"

The King replied, "Those two behaved with kindness, which was meritorious on their part, but the other fought and killed the demon. He brought her back, and therefore she became his wife."

Having heard this, the Baital went and was suspended on the tree, and the King having gone there also, and bound Baital, placed him on his shoulder and thus carried him off.

THE SIXTH TALE

Again the Baital said, "King! There is a city named Dharampur; the King there was named Dharamshil, and his minister's name was Andhak. He said one day to the King, "O great king! Please build a temple; and, having placed in it an image of Devi, offer worship constantly to it. Doing so is described as a very virtuous act in the Shastras."

Then the King, having built a temple, had an image of Devi placed in it, and began to offer adoration, in the manner prescribed by the Vedas. One day the minister said, "O great king! It is proverbial that the house of a man without a son is empty, that the breast of a fool is empty, and everything belonging to a poor man is empty."

Having heard this, the King went into the temple of Devi, and with joined hands began to glorify the goddess, "O Devi! Brahma, Vishnu, Rudra and Indra wait upon you, and you have disdroyed the demon Mahishas, of Chand, Mund, Rakt Bij and other evil spirits, and you have assisted your worshippers, whenever they have been in trouble. It is with this in mind that I have come to the entrance of your temple, fulfil now also the desire of my mind."

When the King had finished thus glorifying Devi, a voice came forth from her temple, "King! I have been pleased with you; ask a boon, whatsoever boon you may desire."

The King said, "O mother! If you have been pleased with me, bestow on me a son."

Devi replied, "King! Your son shall be very powerful and renowned."

Then the King, having made an offering of sandalwood, unbroken rice, flowers, perfumes, lamps, and consecrated food, performed adoration, and was thus in the habit of daily worshipping.

At length, after some days, a son was born to the King, who having gone with music, and rejoicing with his family and kindred, offered adoration to Devi.

It so happened one day that a washerman from a certain city was coming towards this city, accompanied by a friend. Seeing Devi's temple, he resolved to make prostration in it.

In the meantime, he saw a dhobi's (washerman's) daughter, who was exceedingly beautiful, coming by; he was fascinated on seeing her, and went to pay a visit to Devi.

Having joined his hands, he said to himself, "Devi! If through your favour I am married to this beautiful creature, I will make a sacrifice to you of my head."

Having vowed this and bowed his head, he took his friend with him, and went to his own city.

When he arrived there, separated from the object of his love, he forgot sleep, hunger, and thirst, and passed his whole time in meditating upon her.

His friend, perceiving this unfavourable state of affairs, went and explained all the circumstances in detail to his father, who was alarmed. He began to say, "His state appears to be such, that if he should not be betrothed to this damsel, he will abandon life; it is better to marry him to this girl in order that he may escape."

Having thus considered, and taken his son's friend with him, he went to the girl's father, and said to him, "I have come to request something from you."

He replied, "Tell me what you want; and, if I should have the thing, I will give it to you."

Having thus bound him by a promise, the washerman's father said, "Give your daughter to my son."

Having heard and approved of this proposal and called a Brahmin, the day was fixed according to an auspicious time. He said, "Bring your son, and I will also stain my daughter's hands yellow."[4]

Having done this the marriage went ahead and his son and daughter-in-law returned home. The bride and bridegroom began to live happily together.

At marriage, the bride wears yellow garments, stains her hands and feet with turmeric.

After some days, there was another occasion for rejoicing at the house of the daughter's father, and an invitation came for the bride and bridegroom. The husband and wife having made all preparations, and accompanied by their friend, set out for the city. When they arrived, the temple of Devi came into sight, and the circumstances of the vow reoccurred to the washerman.

Having reflected in his mind, he said, "I am a false speaker and have failed in my truth even to Devi." Having uttered these words to himself, he said to his friend, "Stay here, while I go and pay a visit to Devi," and he told his wife to remain there.

Having thus spoken and arrived near the temple, and bathed in an adjoining pool, he went into the presence of Devi. Having joined his hands and addressed her in a reverential manner, he raised his sword and struck himself on the neck, and his head was separated from his body and fell on the ground.

After some delay, his friend thought that he has been gone a long time, so he told his wife to stay where she was and went to search for and find her husband.

He went into Devi's temple and there saw his friend's head, separated from the body, on the ground. On seeing this state of things, he said, "The world is a very difficult place. No one will suppose that my friend has with his own hand offered up his own head to Devi. They will imagine that I have committed this act of treachery and killed him for the purpose of carrying off his wife, who is a very beautiful woman. It is therefore right that I should die here, since it is not proper to submit to a bad reputation in the world."

Having thus spoken, he bathed in a tank and came into Devi's presence, where he joined his hands, raised his sword and struck himself on the neck so that his head was separated from his body. The wife, standing alone in a state of dejection, was waiting for them; and being disappointed at their not coming, went to the temple of Devi to search for them.

On arriving there, she found that they had both fallen dead. She thought to herself, "People will not believe that these two have offered themselves as sacrifices to Devi; all will say, that the widow, in a state of utter perdition, killed them both for the purpose of indulging in debauchery."

Having thus reflected, she dived into the tank and came into the presence of Devi. Bowing her head and making an obeisance, she raised a sword. She was about to strike herself on the neck, when Devi, descending from her throne, laid hold of her with great dignity, and said, "Daughter! Ask a boon, I have been delighted with you."

She replied, "Mother! If you hast been pleased with me, restore these two to life."

The Devi said, "Fasten their heads to their bodies."

She, through joy and fright, exchanged the heads when she fastened them on; and Devi brought and gave them the water of immortality. The two were restored to life, but began to quarrel about whom the wife belonged to."

Having proceeded thus far in the narration, the Baital said, "O King Vikramaditya! To which of these two did the wife belong?"

The King said, "It is laid down in the Shastra, that the Ganges is the most excellent of rivers, and the mountain Sumeru, the most excellent of hills and the Kalpabriksha,[5] the most excellent of trees, and the head is the best part of the body. According to this decision, the wife belonged to him who had the superior head."

Having heard these words, the Baital went and was again suspended on that tree; and the King, having, gone and bound him, and placed him on his shoulder, carried him off.

[5] "Kalpabriksha," a tree in Indra's paradise, which grants whatever, is desired from it.

THE SEVENTH TALE

The Baital said, "King! There is a city named Champapur. The King there was named Champakeshwar and his wife was named Sulochana, and his daughter was named Tribhuwan. She was beautiful; her face was like the moon, her hair like the clouds, her eyes like those of the deer, her eyebrows like a bow. Her nose like a parrot's, her neck like a pigeon's, her teeth, the grains of a pomegranate, the colour of her hands like red fruit, her waist like a leopard's. Her hands and feet like soft lotuses; her complexion like a champa and the splendour of her youth increased daily.

When she was marriageable the King and Queen began to have anxious thoughts; and information reached Kings of different countries, that such a damsel had been born in the house of King Champakeshwar. On beholding her beauty, gods, men and sages were fascinated.

Upon this, Kings of different countries having drawn their picture sent them to King Champakeshwar. The King showed all the pictures to his daughter, but not one of them suited her.

Then the King said, "Select a husband for yourself."

But she did not agree to this either, and said to her father, "Marry me to a man who possesses the excellence of beauty, strength and understanding."

At length four bridegrooms came from four different countries. The King said to them, "Manifest and explain your mental qualities to me."

One of them said, "I can make a cloth and sell it for five rubies and I will give one of the rubies to a Brahmin; the second I offer up to a god. The third I wear on my own person; the fourth I keep for my wife; and, having sold the fifth, I expend the money on entertainment; and my good looks are apparent to everyone."

The second said, "I understand the language of beasts and birds on dry land and the water, and no-one is equal to me in strength, and my beauty is before you."

The third said, "I am so well acquainted with the Shastras that no-one is equal to me in this knowledge, and my beauty you can judge."

The fourth said, "I stand alone in my knowledge of the science contained in the Shastra; there is no-one else like me. I can discharge an arrow, which shall strike what is heard and not seen, and my handsome appearance is notorious throughout the world; you also must now perceive it."

Having heard the speeches of these four persons, the King began to reflect, "To whom shall I give the young girl?" Having thus considered, he went to his daughter and explained the virtues of all four of them to her, and said to her, "To whom shall I give you?"

When she heard these words, she bent her neck through shame and remained silent, and made no reply.

Having narrated thus much, the Baital said, "O King Vikram! Of whom was the young girl worthy?"

The King said, he who made cloth and sold it was a Sudra by caste; and he who understood the language of beasts and birds was of the Baniyah caste. He who had read the Shastra, was a Brahmin; and he who could strike what was heard but not seen was the same caste as the Brahmin; she was a wife worthy of him."

Having heard these words, the Baital went away again, and was suspended on that tree; and the King having gone there, bound him and placing him upon his shoulder, carried him off.

THE EIGHTH TALE

Then the Baital said, "King! There is a city named Mithalawatti and the King was Gunadhip. A Rajput named Chiramdeo came from a distant country to seek employment. He used to go daily to see the King, but failed to get work. In a year all the money he brought with him had gone and his family was ruined.

It happened one day that the King had mounted his horse to go out hunting, and Chiramdeo also accompanied the King's cavalcade. The King was accidentally separated in a forest from his troops, and his attendants also lost their way, so only Chirumdeo remained behind the King.

At length he called out, "O great king! Your attendants cannot go so fast, and I am urging on my horse, and trying to keep up with you."

The King, having heard this, stopped his horse. When the Rajput came up to him, the King, having looked at him, enquired, "How have you become so weak?"

He replied, "It is the fault of a man's own fate, and not the fault of his master. In my opinion, it is better to swallow deadly poison and perish than to ask for money from a great man, who would make faces, or turn up his nose and raise his eyebrows."

The King did not reply, but said to him, "I am hungry, bring me something to eat."

So Chiramdeo went into the jungle and killed a deer. Drawing a flint from his pocket, he lit a fire, broiled some pieces of the flesh, and served up a plentiful meal, which he also ate.

When the King's hunger was satisfied, he said, "Rajput! Take me now to the city, because I do not know the road."

So Chiramdeo took the King to the city and to his royal abode. There the King employed him as a servant, and bestowed many jewels upon him. He began to attend upon the King.

One day the King sent the Rajput to the seashore on some business, and he, seeing a temple of Devi, went and offered adoration to Devi. But when he came thence a beautiful damsel, having followed him began to enquire, "Oh man! Why have you come here?"

He said, "I came for the sake of sexual connection and I am enchanted by your beauty."

She said, "If you have any designs on me, first go and bathe in this pool, and after that I will listen to whatever you say to me."

On hearing these words, having taken off his clothes and gone into the tank and come out of the water, he saw that he was standing in his own city. On beholding this strange sight he was filled with fear, and in despair went home and proceeded to the King's and mentioned all the circumstances.

The King, on hearing them, said, "Show me also this strange sight."

Having sent for his escort they both mounted, and started off. After some days they arrived on the seashore, and having gone into that temple of Devi they offered adoration.

When the King came forth, that damsel came and stood with a female companion near the King; and being fascinated at beholding the handsome appearance of the King, said, "I will execute whatever order you give me."

The King replied to her, "If you will do my bidding, become the wife of my servant."

She said, "I have become the slave of your beauty, how can I become his wife?

The King replied, "You told me just now that you would execute any order I might give you—and good people perform what they promise, do as you said you would and become the wife of my servant."

Having heard this she said, "I approve of what you have said."

Then the King having solemnized a Gandharb[6] marriage between them, took the bride and bridegroom with him and came to his royal abode."

[6] A *Gundhurb* marriage is one when the usual formalities are dispensed with, and the parties by mutual consent only become man and wife, and indeed, these marriages seem often to have resulted more from the will of the man than the consent of the female.

Having related this, the Baital said, "King! Explain whether the virtue of the master or the servant was the greater."

The King said, "The servant's."

The Baital replied, "What! Was not the King's virtue greater, who, having obtained such a beautiful wife, gave her to his servant?"

Then King Vir Vikramaditya said, "What extraordinary merit have they in promoting virtue whose business it is to promote it? But he, who whilst engaged in his own affairs, advances the affairs of others, is a man of superior merit; and therefore, the virtue of the servant was greater than that of his master."

Having heard this the Baital went away, and was suspended on that tree; and the King having gone and taken him down thence, and placed him upon his shoulder, carried him off.

THE NINTH TALE

The Baital said, "King! There is a city named Madanpur, where there was a King named Birbar, and in that country was a Baniyah, named Hirnayadutt, whose daughter's name was Madansena.

One day in the spring season she went into her garden accompanied by her female friends.

It so happened that Somdutt, the son of a merchant, named Dharamdutt, had come before her, to enjoy the forest.

On seeing her, he became fascinated, and began to say to his friend, "Brother! If I obtain her, my life will be prosperous; if not, it is vain for me to live in the world."

Having approached her and seized her hand, he began to say, "If you will not entertain affection for me, I will give up my life for you."

She said, "Please do not do so, as it is a sin to act thus."

He replied, "Your amorous glances have pierced my heart, and the fire of separation from you has burnt up my body."

She said, "Five days hence I am to be married, but first I will have fun with you." Having ratified this promise she went home and the merchant went also.

On the fifth day her marriage took place, and her husband, after the ceremony, took her to his own house. She went and sat silently in a corner of the nuptial chamber. When her husband saw her, he took her hand and seated her on a bed and, when he was on the point of embracing her, she shook him off. She explained to him the promise and agreement she had made with the merchant's son. When her husband heard these things, he said, "If you really desire to go to him, go."

Having received her husband's permission, she went to the merchant's house. A thief saw her on the road and approaching her said, "Where are you going at twelve o'clock at night in the darkness alone, with such a dress and such ornaments?"

She said, "I am going to the place where my dearly beloved lives."

Having heard this the thief said, "Who is here to give you assistance?"

She said, "Madan (Cupid) with a bow and arrows accompanies me to afford protection. Do not destroy my ornaments; I go away, making you a promise that when I return I will make over my ornaments to thee."

When the thief heard this, he said, "She promised to give me her jewels; why should I destroy them?" And with these thoughts he let her go; he sat down there. She went to Somdutt who was asleep.

She awoke him suddenly and he rose in a state of alarm, and began to say, "Are you the daughter of a god, or a demon, or a snake? Say truly, who you are, and why you have come to me."

She said, "I am the daughter of Hirnayadutt.; Madansena is my name; do you not remember how in that grove you seized my hand by force, and insisted on my taking an oath. I took this oath, That I would abandon the man whom I had married, and would come to you? I have come accordingly; do whatever you desire."

He enquired, "Have you told all this to your husband?"

She replied, "I have told him everything and he has allowed me to come to you."

After a full understanding, Somdutt said, "This affair is like jewels without a dress, or food without clarified butter, or singing without melody. These are all alike; thus dirty clothes will put out fire, bad food will destroy strength, a bad wife will destroy life. The deity has created woman a strange being in the world."

Having thus spoken, the merchant's son answered to her, "I have nothing to say to another man's wife."

Having heard these words, she returned home. On the road she met with the thief and told him all the circumstances; when the thief had heard them, he let her go with loud applause.

She came to her husband and explained all the circumstances to him; but her husband showed no affection to her, and said, "The beauty of a cuckoo is its note; chastity is a woman's beauty and forgiveness the beauty of a devotee."

The Baital having related thus much of the story said, "King! Whose virtue was greatest of these three?"

King Vikramaditya said, The thief's was the greatest."

The Baital asked, "Why?"

The King said, "Her husband abandoned her when he saw her affection for another man, and there was no reason why the thief should let her go; and therefore the thief is chief amongst them."

Having heard this the Baital went and was again suspended on that tree, and the King went also and took him down thence; and having bound him, placed him upon his shoulder, and carried him away again.

THE TENTH TALE

Then the Baital said, "King! In the country of Gour, there is a city called Bardwan, and the King's name was Gunshekar. His minister was of the Jain religion and named Abhaychand. He converted the King to the Jain religion.

He prohibited the worship of Shiva and Vishnu, and the giving of gifts of cows, land and balls made of flour or rice. Also gambling and wine. He would not allow anyone in the city to indulge in any of these things. He would not allow anyone to carry away bones to the Ganges. And the minister proclaimed in the city, that if anyone should do any of these prohibited things, the King would confiscate all his property, inflict punishment upon him and expel him from the city.

One day, on another occasion, the minister said to the Rajah, "O great king! Please listen to the judgements and explanations of the Jain religion. Whosoever takes another life, that other takes his life in another world. After he has come into the world, man cannot escape from his sin. He is born again and again; and dies again. For this reason it is right for a man, who has been born in this world, to cultivate religion. Behold! Bramha, Vishnu, and Mahadeo are being under the influence of love, anger, and fascination, descended upon the earth in various ways. But a cow is superior to them all, for it is free from anger, enmity, intoxication, rage, avarice and inordinate affection. It affords protection, and also behaves kindly to and cherishes the animals of the earth. Therefore all the gods and sages regard the cow with respect. In this world, you should respect the cow, for it is virtuous to protect animals. In this world there is no act so impious for men as to eat the flesh of another creature, hereafter all such men fall into hell. It is therefore proper for a man to protect animals. They who do not sympathize with the grief of animals, or kill and eat other animals, do not live long on the earth. They will be born maimed, lame, one-eyed, blind, as dwarfs, hump-backed and deficient. It is a great sin to drink wine and eat flesh and to do so is improper."

The minister, having explained his sentiments to the King, converted him to the Jain religion. So the King ceased to pay respect to Brahmins, yogis, jangans, sanyasis, and dervishes, and carried on his government according to this religion.

One day, being in the power of death, the King departed this life. His son, whose name was Dharam Dhuj, ascended the throne, and began to govern. He called for the minister Abhaychand to be seized. Seven plaits of hair were placed on his head, and his face blackened. He was mounted on a jackass and with a drum beaten before him, he was led round the city and banished.

One day, in the season of spring, the King went to take a stroll in a garden accompanied by his queens. There was a large tank in the garden, in which lotuses were in full bloom. The King took off his clothes and went down to bathe.

Having plucked a flower and come on to the bank, he was in the act of presenting it to one of his queens when the flower escaped from his hand. It fell on to the queen's foot, which was broken by the wound it inflicted.

At this the King became very distressed and began to apply remedies to the wound. At night the moon shone brightly and the falling of the moon's rays blistered the body of another queen. Then, just at the same time, the sound of a wooden pestle came forth from a house where a third queen suffered such pain in her head that she fainted."

Having recited this much of the story, the Baital said, "King! Who was the most delicate of these three queens?"

The King said, "She who fainted in consequence of the great pain in her head."

Having heard these, the Baital went away, and was again suspended on that tree; and the King having gone there, and tied him up in a bundle, placed him upon his shoulder and carried him off again.

THE ELEVENTH TALE

The Baital said, "King! There was a city named Punyapur, whose King's name was Bhima. His minister's name was Satyaprakash and the minister's wife's name was Laxmi.

One day the King said to his minister, "The business of government is unprofitable for a King without a beautiful woman."

Having thus spoken and made over the burden of government to his ministers, he began to indulge in pleasure and amorous delights. He abandoned all cares of the State; and passed his days and nights in enjoyment.

It happened one day that the minister was sitting dejected at his own house, when his wife said to him, "Husband! You seem to me to be weak and emaciated nowadays."

He said, "Day and night I am occupied with anxious thoughts regarding the kingdom; and therefore my body has become weak; and the King is day and night immersed in ease and pleasure."

The minister's wife said, "O husband! You have administered the affairs of State for too long. Take leave now from the Rajah for a few days and go on a pilgrimage."

Having heard this speech of hers, he remained silent; and when he rose thence, he went to the King and, having obtained leave, set out on a pilgrimage.

Proceeding on his journey, he arrived at Setband Rameshwaram[7] on the seashore. He paid a visit to Mahadeo, and

[7] A place of pilgrimage so called from the dyke of stones fabled to have been piled up between Lanka or Ceylon and the mainland, by the monkey army under Hanuman, when he assisted Ram to recover his wife Sita. (*Vide* Shakespeare's Dictionary: Ramchandra.) The cause of the temple to Mahadeo or Shiva being

came forth. When his eyes fell in the direction of the sea he saw a golden tree with leaves of emerald, flowers of topaz, and fruits of coral. It seemed to be exceedingly beautiful, and a very elegant damsel was sitting on the tree with a lute in her hand, singing in sweet soft strains.

After a quarter of an hour the tree disappeared into the sea, and the minister, having seen there this strange sight, returned to his city. Returning to the King, he said, "O great king! I have seen a wonderful thing!"

The King told him to explain and the minister said, "O great king! Men of a former age have told us not to speak of anything which cannot be comprehended and which no-one would believe; but since I have seen this thing clearly with my own eyes, I will mention it. O great king, where Raghunath Ji[8] built a bridge over the sea, I saw a tree of gold with leaves of emerald, flowers of topaz, and fruits of coral. On the tree was a very beautiful woman with a lute in her hand, who was singing sweet strains; but after a quarter of an hour, the tree disappeared into the ocean."

The Rajah, having heard this and having entrusted his government to the minister went alone to the seashore. After some days he arrived there, and went into the temple of Mahadeo to pay him a visit. As he came out, the same tree together with the damsel, came forth from the sea.

On seeing it, the King leapt into the sea, and went and jumped on the tree, which floated away with the King. Then the damsel said unto him, "O brave man! Why have you come here!"

The King replied, "I have come from an eager desire for your beauty."

She replied, "I will marry you, if you will not embrace me on the fourteenth day of the moon in the dark part of the month." The King consented to this; and she married him, having exacted this promise.

When the fourteenth day of the moon in the dark part of the month came, she said, "King! Do not remain near me today."

---

at the place is said to be that as fast as the monkeys completed the dyke, Ravan destroyed it and to prevent this Ram erected a temple. To Shiva, on the end of the dyke, so that Ravan, who was a professional adorer of Shiva, could not destroy that which supported the temple of his tutelary divinity.

[8] Raghunath, a title of Ram or Ramchandra, who being an incarnation of Vishnu, was born in the family of Raghu, he was, of course the chief or Nath of the family.

Having heard this, and taken a sword in his hand, the King rose and went away, but remained looking on in concealment. When it was midnight, a demon came and embraced her.

On seeing this, the King took up his sword and came to the spot and said, "O sinful demon! Do not touch my wife in my presence—first fight with me. I am not afraid of you."

Having thus spoken, and drawn his sword, he struck the demon such a blow, that his head was separated from his body and he began to writhe about on the ground.

When she saw this, she said, "You have done me a great benefit." She proceeded to say, "Rubies are not found in all hills, nor virtuous men in all cities; nor is sandalwood produced in every forest, nor is there a pearl in the head of every elephant.

The King then enquired, "Why did this demon come on the fourteenth day of the moon, in the dark part of the month?"

She said, "My father's name is Bidhyadhar; I am his daughter and my name is Sundari. It was my father's custom not to eat without me being present. One day I was not in the house at his eating time My father became angry and pronounced a curse on me, that a demon should come and embrace me on the fourteenth day of the moon, in the dark part of the month. When I heard this, I said, "Father! You have pronounced a curse, but please show me some kindness." He replied, "You shall be freed from this curse, when a very brave man shall come and kill that demon. I have now been freed from it and will now go and offer a salutation to my father."

The King said, "If you regard my kindness, you will go at once with me and proceed afterwards to pay a visit to your father."

She replied, "I consent to what you have said."

After this the King brought her to his royal residence. Sounds of rejoicing began to be heard; news of the King's arrival spread through the whole city, and then there were songs of congratulation, and festivities in every house. All the musicians and singers in the city came to court and began to offer congratulations.

The King bestowed many gifts, and performed many acts of charity. After some days, the beautiful creature said, "O great king! I will now go to my father."

The King was sad, and said, "Well go."

When she saw that the King was sad she said, "O great king! I will not go."

The King replied, "Why have you given up going to your father's?"

She said, "I now belong to a mortal and my father is a celestial musician. If I were to go now, he would not pay me proper respect, therefore I will not go."

The King was very pleased at hearing this, and made presents, and performed acts of charity costing too many rupees. The minister was much distressed at hearing these circumstances, and he died."

Having related this much, the Baital said, "King! Why did the minister die?"

Then King Vir Vikramaditya said, "This minister saw that the King began to indulge in pleasure and forgot all cares of government, so that his subjects were without a master, and no-one would obey the minister's orders; in consequence of this anxiety he died."

Having heard this the Baital went, and was again suspended on that tree; and the King, having gone there again, placed him in the same manner upon his shoulder, and went away with him.

THE TWELFTH TALE

The Baital said, "King Vir Vikramaditya! There is a city called Churapur, of which the King was Churaman. His spiritual preceptor's name was Deoswami, and his son's name Hariswami, and he was beautiful as Cupid was, and as learned in the Shastras as Brihaspati[9] and as wealthy as Kuvera. He married a Brahmin's daughter named Lajjawatti, and they had great affection for each other.

One night in the hot season they were both fast asleep on the rooftop. The wife's veil fell from her face on one side. A celestial musician, seated in a chariot, was flying in the air when his eyes fell upon her. He brought his chariot down while she was sleeping and flew off with her.

After some delay, the Brahmin also awoke from sleep and, not seeing his wife, was alarmed. He searched throughout the whole house and wandered about in search of her through all the lanes and streets of the city but did not find her anywhere. Then he said to himself, "Who has taken her away and where has she gone?"

At length, when he was in utter despair, he came home grieving. He became quite powerless through excessive grief and restlessness. Having abandoned all household affairs and all the pleasures of the world, wearing only a waistcloth, he went forth on a pilgrimage.

At midday he arrived at a certain city much distressed by hunger and cried, "Give me alms of food. When a man is under the

---

[9] Brihaspati is said to be the preceptor of the gods, and Kuvera the god of riches or wealth.

influence of love, he has no thought of what is right and virtuous, or what he shall eat and drink, and unceremoniously eats his food wherever he finds it."

A Brahmin took his platter from him and, having gone into the house brought it back, filled with rice and milk, and gave it to him. Later he came with it to a pool where there was a large fig tree. Having placed the platter at the roots of the tree, he went into the tank to wash his face and hands. While he was in the water a black snake appeared and thrust his mouth, which was completely filled with poison, into the platter. When the pilgrim returned, having washed his face and hands, he was very hungry indeed.

He ate the milk and rice, and immediately the poison entered into him. He went to the Brahmin and said, "You have given me poison, and I shall soon die from it." Having spoken, he staggered and died.

When the Brahmin saw that he was dead, he turned out his own wife from his house, and said to her, "You, who have murdered a Brahmin, go away." "

Having narrated this much of the story, the Baital said, "King! Who of these three was guilty of the Brahmin's murder?"

The King said, "There is natural poison in a snake's mouth and therefore the snake was not criminal. The Brahmin, thinking that he was hungry, gave him alms of food, and he was also not to be blamed. The man who died ate the milk and rice without knowing that there was poison in it; therefore he was not guilty. The Brahmin's wife gave alms by order of her husband, and was also not at fault. The man who decides the guilty one amongst the four, he himself will be the guilty one. As none is truly guilty."

Having heard this, the Baital returned to the tree, and was suspended on it; and the King, having gone there also, and taken him down thence, bound him, placing him again upon his shoulder, carried him away.

THE THIRTEENTH TALE

The Baital said, "There was a city named Chudrahridaya, and the King of that place was named Randhir. In this city was a merchant named Dharamdhwaj and his daughter's name was Sobhani. Her exceeding beauty and youth increased daily, and her handsome appearance became greater every minute.

It so happened that thefts were being committed constantly at night in that city. When the merchants became annoyed by the thieves they all went in a body to the King, and said to him, "O great king! Thieves have exercised great tyranny in the city, and we cannot remain here."

The King replied, "Well, what has happened, has happened; but you shall not suffer any more annoyance in future—I will make arrangements."

Having thus spoken he brought in many guards and pointed out to them how they should keep watch. He ordered them to put the thieves to death wherever they caught them, without asking any questions.

During the night thefts were still being committed so all the merchants, having again assembled together came to the King and solicited him, "O great king! You have sent watchmen, but still the thieves are not diminished in number and thefts occur daily."

The King replied, "Take leave now, from tonight I will go forth to guard the city."

So the King began to guard the city with a sword and shield alone, and on foot. Having advanced some distance, he saw a thief coming towards him; the King having seen him called out, "Who are you?"

He said, "I am a thief."

The King said, "I am also a thief."

Having heard this, the thief was pleased and said, "Come here and let us go and commit theft together."

Having agreed, the King and the thief stole articles in a great many houses, and came outside the city to a well. Having gone down into the well, they proceeded to the city of the infernal regions.

The thief, having placed the King at the door, took away all the money and valuables to his own house. Meanwhile a female servant came out of his house and, having seen the King, began to say to him, "What has brought you here, O great king! With this wicked man? Well, he shall not come in, run away as far as ever you can, otherwise he will kill you on his arrival."

The King said, "I do not know the road, where shall I go?"

At this, the servant showed him the road back. Later the King, accompanied by all his army, went to the city of the infernal regions by the road of that well, and surrounded the thief's house. And the thief, having come out by another road, went to the master of the city, who was a demon and said, "A King has come to my house to kill me, assist me now or I will abandon your city, and take up my abode in some other."

The demon being pleased at hearing this said, "You have brought food for me, and I am highly pleased with you."

Having said, this, the demon came to the place where the King had surrounded the house with his army, and began to eat men and horses. And when the King saw the figure of the demon, he ran away, and all the persons with whom he ran away escaped, and the demon devoured the rest.

At last, the King was running away alone when the thief came and called out to him, "Are you a Rajput running away from battle?"

On hearing this, the King stood still again and, both confronting each other began to fight. At length the King, having subdued the thief and tied his hands behind his back, brought him into the city. After this, having mounted him on a camel, he sent him all round the city accompanied by a crier.

When the city people saw him they said, "This thief has robbed the whole city and the King will now impale him.

When the thief passed under the house of Dharamdhwaj, the merchant, his daughter having heard the voice of the crier, enquired from her servant, "Why is this proclamation being made?"

She said, "The King has laid hold of the villain and will impale him."

When she heard this, she too ran out to see. On seeing the handsome and youthful thief, she was fascinated. She went to her father and said to him, "Go now to the King and have that thief released."

The merchant replied, "Why should the King release the thief who has pilfered his whole city, and on whose account his whole army has been destroyed?"

Again she said, "Give up all your property to the King and he will have him instantly set free and brought here. If he will not come, I will give up my life."

Having heard this the merchant went to the King and said, "O great king! Please accept five lakhs of rupees from me and release this thief."

The King said, "This thief has robbed the whole city, and on his account my whole army has been destroyed; I will not on any account let him go."

When the King would not consent to what he proposed, the merchant returned home in despair, and said to his daughter, "I said everything that was right and proper to say, but the King would not do what I proposed."

Meanwhile, having taken the thief all round the city, they brought him and made him stand near the impaling stake.

When the thief heard the circumstances of the merchant's daughter, he first burst out laughing heartily, and then began to cry bitterly.

In the meantime, the people pulled him up on to the impaling stake, and the merchant's daughter, having heard of his death, came to that place to offer herself as a sacrifice (performing satti). Having made a funeral pyre, she took down the thief from the impaling stake and, having placed his head on her lap, she sat down to be burnt, and ordered the pyre to be kindled.

It so happened that there was a temple of Devi nearby. The Devi quickly came forth and said, "Daughter! I am gratified at seeing your resolution; ask a boon from me."

She said, "Mother! If you have been pleased with me, restore this thief to life."

Devi replied, "It shall be so." Having thus spoken and brought the water of immortality from the regions below, she restored the thief to life."

Having proceeded this far in the narrative, the Baital enquired, "King! Explain why the thief first laughed, and afterwards cried."

The King said, "I know the reason why he laughed, and I know also why he cried; listen to me, Baital."

"He thought to himself that she had fallen in love with him, when he was on the point of death. How strange, the nature of God is not to be understood. He bestows wealth on a man of ill omen, science on a man of inferior family, a beautiful wife on a fool, and pours down rain on hills. Thinking on these things, the thief laughed. Then the thief thought in his mind that he could not perform any act of kindness towards her who was willing to give up everything for his sake and therefore he shed tears."

Having heard this, the Baital went away, and was again suspended on that tree. The King went there and, having untied him, made a bundle of him, placed him upon his shoulder, and carried him off.

THE FOURTEENTH TALE

The Baital said, "King Vikram! There was a city named Kusmawati, the King of which was Subchar, whose daughter's name was Chandraprabha. When she became marriageable, she went one day in the spring to stroll in the garden with her female companions. Before this a very handsome son of a Brahmin, named Maswi, had came wandering about in the garden, and had fallen asleep in a cool shady place under a tree.

The King's people made apartments for the ladies; but it so happened that no one had observed the Brahmin's son sleeping under the tree. The King's daughter went into the garden with her attendants and, wandering about with her companions, came to the spot where the Brahmin's son was sleeping.

On her arrival he woke and sat up; their eyes met, and they were so under the influence of love that Maswi fell down in a swoon on the ground, and the King's daughter was in a state of unconsciousness, and her feet began to tremble.

Seeing this, her companions supported her in their arms and, having at length placed her in a recumbent posture in a litter, they brought her home. The Brahmin's son had fallen down in such a state of insensibility as to be altogether unconscious of everything.

Just at this time two Brahmins, named Shashi and Muldeo, learned men, arrived at the spot. Muldeo, having perceived that the Brahmin's son had fallen down, said, "Shashi, why has this man fallen down in such a state?"

He replied, "A damsel has shot forth the arrows of her eyes, from the bow of her eyebrows, and therefore he has fallen down."

Muldeo said, "We must raise him up."

He replied, "What need is there for you to raise him up?"

Muldeo did not approve of what Shashi said, and sprinkled water on him and lifted him up, and enquired, "What has been the matter with you?"

Upon this Maswi said, "We should tell our grief to one who can remove it; what is gained by telling it to one, who, after having heard them, cannot remove it?"

He replied, "Well, tell me your troubles, and I will remove them."

So Maswi said, "A King's daughter came with her companions and I fell in love. If I obtain her I will continue to live, if not I will die."

Then he continued, "God has created many jewels on the earth, but the jewel of woman is the best of all, and for her sake man desires wealth; what is the use of money to a man who has no wife? Animals are superior in the world to those who have not obtained beautiful wives. The fruit of virtue is wealth, and the fruit of wealth is ease, and the fruit of ease is woman; and where woman is not, how can there be happiness?"

Having heard these remarks Muldeo said, "I will give you whatever you ask."

Maswi said, "O Brahmin! Procure for me that damsel."

Muldeo replied, "Come with me, and I will procure her for you."

In short, having offered him great comfort, he took him away to his own house. There he made up two balls. Having given one of the balls to Maswi he said, "When you put this into your mouth, you will become a young girl of twelve years of age. So he did, and he became a young girl of twelve years of age, and, having placed the other ball in his own mouth, Muldeo was changed into an old man of eighty years of age. He took the young girl with him to the King who, having seen the Brahmin, made a salutation and offered both a seat.

Then the Brahmin repeated the following text, the beauty of which has spread throughout three worlds, "May the Vasudeo[10] protect you, who as a dwarf deceived King Bali[11] , and who, having

[10] Vasudeo—a form of Vishnu.

[11] King Bali was a good and powerful king, who by austerities and devotion had overcome Indra in battle and obtained power both in heaven and earth. The gods became fearful of his subverting their reign, and applied to Vishnu, who

taken monkeys with him, made a bridge over the sea, and supported a hill in his hand and saved the cowherd's children from the thunderbolts of Indra!"

Having heard this, the King enquired, "O great king! From where do you come?"

Muldeo, the Brahmin, said, "I have come from the other side of the Ganges. I had gone to bring my son's wife and after this a general emigration took place from my village, and I know not where my wife and son have fled. How can I search for them now, having this damsel with me? It is, therefore, better that I should leave her with you until my return; take great care of her."

Having heard the speech, the King began to reflect in his mind, "How shall I be able to take care of a very beautiful young woman; if I do not take care of her, this Brahmin will curse me, and my government will be utterly destroyed."

Having reflected, the King said, "O great king! I consent to what you have directed me to do."

Then the King having sent for his daughter said, "Daughter! Take this Brahmin's daughter-in-law to your own apartment, and show her great care and attention, and allow her not to be separated from you for a single moment whether asleep or awake, eating, drinking, walking, or wandering about.

Having heard this, the King's daughter laid hold of Maswi, the Brahmin's daughter-in-law, and took her away to her own house. At night both slept in one bed, and began to converse with each other. In the course of conversation Maswi said, "O royal damsel! Tell me through what grief you have become emaciated?"

The King's daughter said, "I had gone one day in the spring, accompanied by my female companions, to take a stroll in a garden. There I saw a exceedingly handsome Brahmin, equal to Kamdeo (Cupid), and his eyes met mine. He became senseless, and I lost all consciousness. Now I have no appetite for eating or drinking; from this pain my body has been reduced to this state."

---

descended on the earth as a dwarf (*Baman Avatar*) Brahman. In this shape he waited on Bali, who according to custom, offered him large presents. The dwarf, under pretence of total contempt of worldly things, refused, and said he only wanted space for three steps. Buli laughed and promised him his desire. On receiving his promise, the dwarf's stature increased prodigiously so that at one step he placed his food on the heavens, at the next step, he rested his foot on Bali's head and thus sunk down to Naglok, a region beneath the earth, where he was confined, being bound by rope made a twisted serpents.

Having heard this, Maswi said, "If I shall procure your beloved for you, what will you give me?"

The King's daughter replied, "I will always remain your servant."

Having heard this, Maswi took the ball out of his mouth, and "she" became a man again and the daughter was abashed at beholding him.

After that Maswi married her according to the customs of Ghandharb[12] marriages, and at night he constantly became a man and in the day times a woman. At length, after six months, the King's daughter became pregnant.

It happened one day that the King went with all his relations to a marriage at the house of his minister, where the minister's son saw Maswi in the disguise of a woman.

On seeing her he fell in love, and said to one of his friends, "If I do not obtain this woman, I will give up my life."

At this time the King came home with his family. The minister's son's state became most distressing from the burning flame of separation from her he loved, and he gave up food and water.

A friend, having perceived the state he was in, went and told the minister of it, who having heard the circumstances, proceeded to the King, and said, "My son is distracted, O great king! With the love of the Brahmin's daughter-in-law; he has given up eating and drinking, if you will compassionately give her to me, his life will be saved."

The King was angry when he heard this and said, "You fool! It is not right for Kings to commit such injustice. Is it right to give away her who has been entrusted to me by another without obtaining the permission of the person who entrusted her to my care?"

The minister, on hearing these words, went home hopeless; but having beheld his son's affliction, he also gave up food and water. When the minister had spent three days without eating and drinking all the courtesans gathered together and represented to the King, "O great king! The minister's son is in a precarious way and if he dies, the minister will not survive; and if the minister dies, the affairs of the kingdom will not continue to be well administered; it is better that you should agree to our solicitation."

Having heard this, the King gave them permission to say what they required. Then one amongst them said, "O great king! It

[12] *Vide* footnote 6, *Page* 44-45

is long since told that a Brahmin went away and he has not as yet returned. God knows whether he is dead or alive; it is therefore proper that you should confirm your government by giving that Brahmin's daughter-in-law to the minister's son. If he should come you can bestow wealth on him; if he should not be pleased with this, you can celebrate his son's marriage[13] and allow him to take leave."

Having heard this speech the King, having summoned Maswi, said, "Go to the house of my minister's son."

She replied, "The virtue of a woman is destroyed by her possessing excessive beauty, and the religion of a Brahmin is impaired by attendance on a King and a cow is spoilt by a distant pasture. Wealth is lost by committing acts of injustice." She proceeded to say, "If, O great king! You will give me to the minister's son, be pleased to exact from him this one thing, that he will do whatever I tell him, and then I will go to his house."

The King said, "Say what he will have to do."

She replied, "O great king! I am of the Brahmin caste, and he is a Kshetri; it is therefore advisable that he should first visit all places of pilgrimage, and then I will cohabit with him."

When the King heard this speech he sent for the minister's son, and said to him, "Go first to all places of pilgrimage, and then we will give the Brahmin's girl to thee."

Having heard the King's speech, the minister's son said, "O great king; let her go and remain in my house, and then I will go on pilgrimage."

Having heard this, the King said to Maswi, "If you will first go and stay in his house, he will proceed on a pilgrimage."

The Brahmin's girl having no alternative after the King's speech went and dwelt in the minister's son's house. He said to his wife, "You must both remain together in one place on terms of the greatest affection and friendship, and not have any kind of dispute or contention with each other, and you must not go into any strange house."

Having given these instruction, he went on pilgrimage and his wife, named Saubhagya Sundari, having taken Maswi with her, began to talk to her on various subjects.

---

[13] The meaning is, if the old Brahmin should on his return be angry at his daughter-in-law having been married to the Minister's son, you can provide another wife for the old man's son.

After some delay the minister's son's wife said, "O friend! At this time I am being burnt up with desire, but how shall I gain my object?"

The other replied, "What will you give me, if I accomplish your objective for you!"

She said, "I will always be subservient to you, standing in your presence with joined hands."

Then Maswi, having taken the ball out of his mouth, was transformed into a man. He thus constantly became a man at night and a woman in the daytime and these two had great love for each other. In short, six months passed away in this manner until the minister's son returned.

When people heard the news of his arrival, they began to indulge in festive rejoicing, and Maswi, having taken the ball out of his mouth and being transformed into a man, went away from the female apartments through a window. After some delay, he arrived at the house of Brahmin Muldeo, who had given him the ball, and mentioned to him the circumstances of his transformation.

Then Muldeo, having heard all the circumstances and taken away the ball from him, gave it to his companion, the Brahmin Shashi, and they both put the balls in their mouths.

Muldeo was transformed into an old man and Shashi into a man of twenty. The two went again to the King, who, having made a salutation on seeing them, offered them seats. They also gave him their benedictions.

The King, having made inquiries regarding their health and welfare, said to Muldeo, "Where have you been for so many days past?"

The Brahmin relied, "O great king! I went to search for this my son, and having been successful in my search, I have brought him to you; give me now my daughter-in-law, and I will take her and my son to my house."

The King related to the Brahmin all that had occurred. The Brahmin was exceedingly angry on hearing the circumstances and said to the King, "What is this that has happened, that you have given my son's wife to another man? Well, you have done what you wished, but now receive my curse."

The King replied, "O divinity! Be not angry, whatever you say I will do."

The Brahmin said, "If from a fear of my curse you will do as I say, marry your daughter to my son."

The King having heard this, having sent for an astrologer and fixed on an auspicious moment, married his daughter to the Brahmin's son, Shashi, who returned home to his village with the King's daughter and her dowry.

When Maswi heard the news of these events, he came there and began to quarrel with him, and asked him to give up his wife, claiming her as his own.

The Brahmin Shashi said, "This is my wife, and I have brought her here after having married her in front of five or ten persons."

He replied, "She is with child by me, how can this woman be your wife?"

And they began to carry on an altercation with each other. Muldeo reasoned a great deal with them both, but neither of them assented to what he said."

When he related thus much of the story, the Baital said, "King Vir Vikramaditya! Say whose wife she was."

The King replied, "She was the wife of the Brahmin Shashi."

Baital said, "How could she be his wife, having become pregnant by Maswi?"

The King replied, "No-one knew that Maswi had got her with child, and Shashi married her in the presence of many other persons. Therefore she became his wife, and that child will also be entitled to perform his funeral obsequies."

Having heard these remarks, the Baital went off, and was suspended in that tree; and the King went again, and having bound the Baital, placed him upon his shoulder and carried him off.

THE FIFTEENTH TALE

The Baital said, "King! There is a hill named Himalchali. There is a city of celestial musicians, where King Jimutketu governed. On one occasion he offered great adoration to the Kalpabriksha[14], praying for a son.

The spirits of the tree, being pleased, said to him, "I am gratified by your assiduous attendance; ask any boon that you wish."

The King replied, "Give me a son, in order that my Government and name may continue."

The tree spirit said, "It shall be so."

After some time, the King had a son. He was highly delighted, gave very many gifts, performed many acts of charity, and sent for Brahmins to give him a name. The Brahmins named him Jimutbahan.

When he was twelve years of age he began to offer worship to Shiva. Having read all the Shastras, he became very learned, contemplative, bold, resolute, brave, religious, and wise. At that time there was no one equal to him, and under his government all his subjects were attentive to their moral and religious duties.

When he became a young man, he was very assiduous in performing religious service to the Kalpabriksha, and the tree, being greatly pleased, and said to him, "Ask me for whatsoever you desire, and I will grant it to you."

Jimutbahun replied, "If you are pleased with me, remove the poverty of all my subjects, and make all persons under my government equal in property and wealth."

---

[14] *Vide* footnote 5, *Page* 40

Upon this the Kalpabriksha granted the boon; all men were so plentifully supplied with wealth, and so much at their ease, that no one obeyed another's order.

When the subjects of that government had arrived at this state, the brothers and relatives of the King began to reason amongst themselves, "that the father and son were both obedient to the dictates of religion, and that their subjects would not obey their orders. It is therefore a most advisable measure to seize and imprison them both and take away the government from them."

The King did not trouble himself to adopt any precautions against them, and they conspired together; and, taking an army with them went and surrounded the King's house.

When news of this reached the King, he said to his son, "What shall we do now?"

The son replied, "O great king! Please remain here; by favour of your virtuous qualities I will go immediately and destroy them."

The King said, "Son! This body is frail and wealth too is unstable; when a man is born, death is also with him; it is therefore right to abandon government and to cultivate virtue and religion."

To this his son replied, "Well, please give your government to your relatives, and go yourself and perform acts of austere devotion."

Having determined on this, the King went with his son to the top of Himalchali Mountain and began to live in a cottage, which they built there.

Jimutbahan was friendly with the son of a sage. One day he and the sage's son had gone to walk about on the top of the hill and saw there a temple of Bhawani.

In the temple there was a King's daughter with a lute in her hand, singing in the presence of Devi. Jimutbahan met her gaze and they fell in love. But the King's daughter, restraining her passion, left and spent the night in a state of great restlessness.

In the morning the King's daughter went to the temple of Devi, and the King's son, on his arrival, found her there. He then enquired from one of her attendants, "Whose daughter is this?"

The attendant replied, "This is the daughter of King Malyaketu; her name is Malyawatti, and she is still a virgin."

Having spoken, the attendant enquired from the King, "Say; O handsome man! From where have you come, and what is your name?"

He said, 'I am the son of Jimutketu, the King of the celestial dancers, and my name is Jimutbahan; our government having been taken from us, we have both, father and son, come and taken up our abode here."

When the attendant heard these things, he mentioned them all to the King's daughter, who, having heard them, was greatly grieved. Her attendants explained all the circumstances to her mother, who mentioned them to the King, and said, "O great king! Your daughter is marriageable, why do you not look out for a bridegroom for her?"

The King, having heard this, sent for his son Mittrabassu and said to him, "Son! Look out for a bridegroom for your sister, and bring him here."

He replied, "I have heard, O great king! That Jimutketu, King of the celestial dancers, and his son Jimutbahan, having abandoned their kingdom, have both come here."

Upon hearing this, King Malyaketu said, "I will give my daughter to Jimutbahan." With these words he instructed his son to go and bring Jimutbahan to his house.

He went to the house and said to Jimutketu, "Allow your son to accompany me, my father has sent for him to bestow his daughter upon him.

Having heard this, King Jimutketu allowed his son to accompany him, and the son came to the King Malyaketu's house and the King celebrated his marriage in the Gandharb manner.

When his marriage was complete, the King brought the bride and Mittrabassu to his house; the three then saluted the King, who gave them his blessing. The day passed away thus. On the morning of the second day, both the son and son-in-law went forth to wander about on the Malyagir hill[15]; when they went there, Jimutbahan saw a rather lofty white heap, and said to his brother-in-law, "How is it, brother, that we see this white heap?"

He replied, "From the regions below come tens of millions of young snakes, whom the bird, on which Vishnu rides,[16] comes here and devours; this is a heap of their bones."

---

[15] This hill has already been called Malyachul, but "Achal" and giri both signify hill or mountain and Mulya is the actual name; it is a hill south of the Narmada and in Sanskrit poetry is spoken of as the abode of the cool southerly breezes.

[16] Garur, represented as a gigantic bird with the face of a man, the "Bahan" or vehicle of Vishnu, —he is the elder brother of Indra, being the produce of the second egg laid by Vanita, daughter of Dukhya after her marriage with Kashyap,

Having heard this, Jimutbahan said to his brother-in-law, "Friend! Go home and eat, because at this time, I am in the constant habit of performing worship and the time for doing so has now come."

When he heard this, he went away, and Jimutbahan proceeded onwards, when the noise of weeping began to reach him.

When he heard it he proceeded, and there saw an old woman greatly agitated by grief, and weeping. He went up to her and enquired, "Mother! Why are you weeping?"

She said, "The snake Sankhchur is my son, and it is his turn today. Garur will come and eat him up. I am weeping on account of this."

He replied, "Mother! Weep not, I will give my own life in exchange for your son's."

The old woman said, "Son! Do not do so, you are my Sankhchur."

While she was speaking, Sankhchur came there also, and having heard what had passed, said, "O great king! Many poor wretches like me are born and have died; but just and compassionate men like you are not born every hour in the world. Do not therefore give up your life instead of mine, because hundreds of thousands of men will benefit by your living, and my living or dying are both the same."

Jimutbahan replied, "It is not consistent with the virtue of men of truth not to do as they say; go back to the place you came from."

Having heard this, Sunkhchoor went to visit Devi. In the meanwhile, Guroor came down from the sky. The prince saw that his legs were each equal to four bamboo in length, his beak as long as a palm tree, his belly like a hill, his eyes like gates, and his feathers like clouds.

All at once he rushed with open beak upon the King's son, who saved himself the first time. The second time the bird flew off with him in his beak, and began to make circuits in the air; in the meanwhile a bracelet, on the stone of which the King's name was engraved became unfastened and fell down covered with blood in front of the King's daughter. On seeing it she fainted and fell.

---

who was the father, of the gods by another of his wife's name Aditya. The foregoing will account for Guroor's having power to bring the water of immortality from the regions under the earth.

When she had recovered her senses, she communicated by a message all the circumstances to her father and mother, who came there when they heard of this calamity. When they saw the bracelet covered with blood, the three set out to search for Jimutbahan. On the road, they also met Sankhchur, who went alone in advance of them to the place where she had seen the prince, and began calling out and saying, "O Garur! Let him go; he is not your food, my name is Sankhchur, I am your food.

Garur was frightened at hearing this and fell down, thinking to himself that he had devoured a Brahmin or a Kshetri.

He then began to say to Jimutbahan, "O man! Say truly why you give up your life."

The prince replied, "O Garur! Trees spread their shade over others, and being themselves exposed to the sun, produce flowers and fruits for other's sake; this is the excellence of good men and of trees. What is the use of this body if it is not serviceable to others? The best men do not abandon their good dispositions even with their lives; what does it matter if men praise or blame them, or if they have wealth or not? Or what does it signify if they die now or after a time? Just men never deviate from their path, happen what may. A man's life is fruitless, whose body is not of benefit to others. The dog and the crow cherish their own lives only, whereas Brahmins, who sacrifice life for the sake of others, dwell certainly and forever in paradise."

Garur said, "In the world all men cherish their own life, and there are very few who give up their own lives to save the lives of others." He proceeded to say, "Ask a boon from me, I have been gratified by the resolution."

Having heard this, Jeemootbahun said, "O divinity! If you are pleased with me, do not eat snakes any more and restore to life those you have already eaten."

When Garur heard this, he brought the water of immortality from the regions below, and sprinkled it on the bones of the snakes, and they were restored to life. Then he said to the King, "O Jimutbahan! Through my favour you shall obtain your lost government."

Having granted this boon, Garur went to his own abode and Sankhchur likewise and Jimutbahan went to theirs. On the road he met his father-in-law, mother-in-law and his wife, and went with them to his father's place.

When they heard of his approach, his uncle and cousins and all his relations came out to meet him, and having fallen at his feet and taken him away with them, they seated him on the throne."

Having related this much of the story, the Baital enquired, "King! Whose virtue was greatest amongst these?"

King Vir Vikramaditya said, "Sankhchur's."

Baital enquired, "Why so?"

The King replied, "She came and gave life to the King who had lost it, and saved him from being eaten by Garur."

The Baital said, "Why was not his virtue greatest who gave his life for another's sake?"

The King said, "Jimutbahan was a Kshetri by caste, and it was therefore his practice to give up his life; hence to give it up was not a difficult matter for him."

Having heard this, the Baital went up and was again suspended on the tree, and the King having gone there and bound him, placed him upon his shoulder, and carried him off.

THE SIXTEENTH TALE

The Baital said, "King Vir Vikramaditya, there is a city Chandrashekar, where lived Ratandatt, a great merchant, who had a daughter named Unmadini.

When she had reached the age of puberty, her father went to the King of that place and said, "O great king! In my house there is a young girl; if you have any wish for her, be pleased to take her, otherwise I will give her to someone else."

Having heard this, the King sent for two or three old servants and said to them, "Go and examine the features of this merchant's daughter."

They came to the merchant's house and all of them were fascinated at the lovely appearance of the damsel. Her beauty was like a light in a dark house; her eyes were like those of a deer; her curls like female snakes; her eyebrows like a bow; her nose like a parrot's. Her teeth were like a string of pearls, her lips like the red ground; her neck like a pigeon's; her waist like a leopard's, her hands and feet like a soft lotus with her face as bright as the moon, of the colour of the champa flower with the gait of the goose, and the voice of a koel[17], on seeing whose beauty and the courtezans of Indra would have been bashed,

Having beheld such an elegant creature, they thought, "If such a woman should go to the King's house, the King would become her slave, and would not cast a thought on the affairs of government. Therefore it would better to tell the King that she was ugly and not worthy of him."

---

[17] The Indian cuckoo. A bird quite familiar to every traveller in India,

Having thus reflected and returned to the King's house, they brought these tidings, "O great king! We have seen that girl, and she is not worthy of you."

The King having heard this, said to the merchant, "I will not marry her."

Upon this the merchant, having come home, married his daughter to Balbhaddra, who was the King's commander-in-chief, and she began to live in his house.

It happened one day that the King went out with his attendants and she was standing on the roof of her house. The King met her eyes accidentally and he began to say to himself, "Is this the daughter of a divinity, or a celestial courtesan, or the child of a mortal?"

In short, he was fascinated with her beauty and came back to his own house in a state of very great agitation.

When the doorkeeper saw his face, he said, "O great king! What pain are you suffering?"

He said, "As I was proceeding along the road today, I saw a very beautiful woman on a rooftop; I don't know her, but she is lovely and bewitched my mind at once. This is why I am restless."

Having heard this the doorkeeper told the King that she was the merchant's daughter, who had married his commander-in-chief, Balbhaddra."

The King said, "The people whom I sent to examine her features have deceived me." Having thus spoken, the King ordered a chobdar[18] to bring those people quickly to him.

When they came into the King's presence, the King said, "You did not execute the commission I gave you, nor did you fulfil my desire, but brought me back an answer having invented a falsehood. Today I have seen her with my own eyes; she is so beautiful and so replete with good qualities that to meet with any woman like her is difficult."

When they heard this, they said, "O great king! What you say is true, but please listen to the reason we said she was ugly. We thought that if such a beautiful woman came to you, you would be completely under her influence and would abandon all affairs of state. The government would be utterly ruined, from fear of this we made the excuse we did."

---

[18] An attendant who bears a silver or gold stick, "chob" as the mark of his office.

The King replied to them that they spoke the truth, but now, just thinking of her, he was in a state of the greatest uneasiness. The King's agitation was manifest to everyone. Meanwhile Balbhaddra came there also and, having joined his hands, standing in the King's presence said to him, "O lord of the earth! I am your servant, and she is your servant, and why should you suffer so much on her account? Be pleased to give orders that she should be brought here."

The King was exceedingly angry at hearing this speech and said, "It is a very irreligious act to go near another man's wife. What is this that you have said to me? Do you think me devoid of religion that I should commit this act? Another man's wife is like a mother. Hear me, brother, a man should regard the souls of other men in the same light as he regards his own."

Balbhaddra said, "She is my servant; when I have given her to you, how can she be another man's wife? The King replied, "I will not commit an act through which scandal would be attached to me." The commander-in-chief then said to the King that he would turn her out of his house and keep her in another place, and having made a prostitute of her, bring her to the King.

The King said, "If you make a virtuous woman a harlot, I will inflict great punishment on you." Having spoken, the King, occupied with the recollection of her, died ten years later.

Then Balbhaddra, the commander-in-chief went to his spiritual preceptor and enquired, "What must I do, please instruct me, as my master has died for the sake of Unmadini."

He said, "It is a virtuous act for a servant to sacrifice his own life after his master's."

Having heard this, he went joyfully to the place where they had taken away the King to burn him. Whilst the King's funeral pyre was being made ready, he finished bathing and offered up prayers. When they lit the pyre, he approached it and, having joined his hands, facing the sun, began to say, "O divine sun! This is in every respect the most earnest and sincere desire of my mind, that in every succeeding birth I may meet with this master, and celebrate with songs your excellent qualities."

Having thus spoken, and made a salutation, he leapt into the fire. When Unmadini heard this, she went to her spiritual preceptor and enquired, "O great preceptor, what is it right for a wife to do in this case?"

He said, "She is a chaste woman and a woman of pure descent who serves him to whom her father and mother have given him (their daughter). And it is thus written in the Dharma Shastra, 'That a woman who in her husband's lifetime engages in devotion and fasts, shortens her husband's days, and hereafter falls into hell. It is best to serve and attend on a husband, however deficient he may be, as a woman gains salvation by doing so. And whatsoever woman forms a desire of sacrificing herself on a funeral pyre in a place where bodies are burnt, there cannot be a doubt that the same paces she takes in advancing towards the pile, as is derived by the sacrifice of a horse.[19] And there is no act so virtuous for a woman to perform as to sacrifice herself on a funeral pyre.'"

Having heard this, and made a salutation, and having bathed and engaged in meditation and bestowed many gifts on Brahmins, she approached the pyre, and having gone once round to the right by way of adoration, said, "O Lord! I am your servant in each succeeding birth." Having spoken, she too went and sat in the fire and was burnt."

Having proceeded this far in the narrative, the Baital said, "King! Whose virtue was the greatest of these three?"

King Vir Vikramaditya said, "The King's." The Baital enquired how it was so.

The King said, "He resigned the wife of the commander-in-chief, who had been given to him, and sacrificed his life for her, but maintained his virtue. It is the duty of a servant to give up his life for his lord, and it is proper for a wife to sacrifice herself on a funeral pyre for the sake of her husband; and, therefore, the King's virtue was the greatest."

Baital, having heard this much, went and was suspended on that tree, and the King also having followed him, bound him again, placed him upon his shoulder, and took him away.

"Ashwamedh" is one performed only by powerful kings, involving vast expense, and is supposed to be of the highest efficacy far excelling all common sacrifice.

THE SEVENTEENTH TALE

The Baital said, "King, there was a King of the city of Ujjain, named Mahasen. One Deosharma Brahmin was an inhabitant of the place and his son's name was Gunakar. The son was a great gambler, to such an extent that he lost all the Bràhmin's wealth in gambling. Then all the members of the family expelled Goonakur from their house, and he was unable to do anything.

Being in despair, and without resources, he left and came to a certain city. After some days he saw a yogi sitting over a fire and imbibing smoke by way of penance. Having made a salutation to the holy man, he also sat down.

The yogi enquired from him, "Will you eat anything?"

He said, "Yes if you will give me something to eat?"

The yogi, having filled a human skull with food, brought it and gave it to him, who, on seeing it, said, "I will not eat food from this skull."

When the yogi saw that he did not eat anything, he read such an incantation that a female spirit made its appearance, and with joined hands said, "O great king! I will do whatsoever you may order."

The yogi said, "Give this Brahmin such food as he desires."

When she heard this, she built a fine house, and placed in it all the requisites for pleasure and enjoyment. She applied sandal with rosewater to his body.

Then she gave him fine clothes, which had been scented with perfume. And having cast a garland of flowers around his neck took him and placed him on a bed.

Meanwhile evening came, and she, adorning herself, came and sat down on the bed with the Brahmin and passed the whole night with pleasure and enjoyment.

When it was morning, the female spirit went off to her own abode, and he came to the yogi and said, "Master, she has gone away, what shall I do now?"

The yogi replied, "She came here through the power above, and remains with him who is possessed of all knowledge."

He said, 'O great king! Grant me this knowledge that I may become gradually familiarised to it."

The yogi then gave him a charm and said, "Sit in water at midnight for forty days, and learn this charm with undivided attention."

When the forty days had elapsed, he came to the yogi and said, "O great king! I have been learning the charm for the number of days you told me to do so."

He said, "Practise it now for the same number of days, sitting in fire."[20]

He replied, "O great king! I will pay one visit to my family, and will then come and practise it."

Having thus spoken to the yogi, he went home, and his relations on seeing him, embraced him and began to weep. His father said, "O Gunakar! Where have you been for so many days past and why have you forgotten your home?" Whoever abandons and remains separated from a chaste wife or turns his back upon a youthful one, or who does not love her who loves him, is on a level with a man of low caste." And it is said, "That the practice of the domestic virtues is not equalled by any other virtue. There is not any woman in the world that can confer happiness equal to one's own wife. They who treat their father and mother with scorn will never obtain salvation," this Brahmin has said.

Guṇakar replied, "This body is composed of blood and flesh, and is food for worms and its excellence is such, that if one neglects it for a day, it begins to stink. They are fools who have affection for such a body, and they are wise who have not friendship for it. And this is the virtue of his body that it repeatedly dies. However much a man may purify his body; it will not become clean. Like an earthen pot filled with dirt, washing the outside only will not make it clean."

[20] It is a common practice with devotees, who practise austerities to sit during the hot months surrounded by chaffing dishes containing fire.

Having thus spoken, he took leave of his home, came to the yogi, sat down in fire and practised the charm. But the female spirit did not come. So he went to the yogi, who said to him, "You have not obtained knowledge," and he said that he had not.

Having related this much of the story, the Baital said, "Say, King, why he did not obtain knowledge."

The King replied, "The devotee was of a wavering mind and therefore did not obtain it. It has been said that a charm is accomplished when a person is of one mind, and never when he wavers." He continued, "That whatever power or ability a man may display, fate accompanies him, and whatever he may do of his own understanding, only that which is written in his fate is obtained by him."

Having heard this, the Baital went to the tree again, and was suspended on it, and the King, having followed and bound him, placed him on his shoulder, and took him away.

THE EIGHTEENTH TALE

The Baital said, "King, there was a city named Kukalpur, in which dwelt King Sudache and a rich merchant. The merchant's name was Dhanchi and he had a daughter by name Dhanwatti. While she was very young, he married her to a Baniyah, named Gauridutt.

After some time she had a daughter, whom she named Mohani. When she was a certain age, her father died; and the Baniyah's relations took away all the property. She, in despair, proceeded during the darkness of night to the house of her father-in-law. Having gone a short distance she lost the road and came to a cemetery where a thief was stuck on a stake. All of a sudden her hand touched his foot.

The thief said, "Who has given me pain just now?"

She replied, "I have not given you pain intentionally, forgive me."

He said, "No mortal gives pain and pleasure to another; whatever the Supreme Being writes in a man's fate. Men are bound in the thread of fate, which draws them away in any direction it pleases. The acts or the nature of the Supreme Being cannot be understood. Men imagine one thing in their minds and the Deity brings another thing to pass."

Having heard this, Dhanwatti asked him who he was and he said, "I am a thief; this is the third day I have been on this impaling stake, and I have not died."

She enquired why and he replied, "I am unmarried; if you will give your daughter to me in marriage, I will give you ten million gold mohurs."

It is well known that greed is the root of sin, and passion the origin of pain, and affection the origin of sorrow. Whoever abandons these three will be happy.

At last Dhanwatti from greed gave her daughter to the thief, and said to him inquiringly, "I desire that you should have a son, but how can this be?"

He said, "When she reaches the age of puberty, send for a handsome Brahmin and give him five hundred gold mohurs and she will thus have a son."

Having heard these words, Dhanwatti gave her daughter four turns around the stake and married her to the thief, who then said to her, "There is tree near a large well of masonry in the eastern quarter, beneath which those gold mohurs have been buried; go and take them."

When he had spoken, he died. She went and took away a few gold mohurs from the heap, and came to her mother and father's house.

Having heard this, she brought a Brahmin to the mother, who on seeing him said, "Oh Brahmin! My daughter is young, if you will stay with her, I will give you a hundred gold mohurs for a son."

When he heard this he said that he would remain with her.

While they were conversing, she gave him delicacies. Now a well-known proverb says, "Enjoyment is of eight kinds; first, perfume; second, a woman; third dress; fourth singing; fifth, pawn; sixth food; seventh, the couch; eighth, ornaments," and all these were found there.

When three hours of the night had been spent, he went to an apartment dedicated to voluptuous enjoyment, and passed the whole night with her in joyful pleasures. At dawn of day he went to his own house, and she arose and came to her companions, one of whom asked her what pleasures she had been enjoying with her lover."

She said, "When I went and sat near him I felt a kind of palpitation; but when he smiled and laid hold of my hand I was quite overcome by him, and I cannot say what happened."

And it is been said, "A woman never forgets either in this birth or a succeeding one. Firstly, a husband of reputation; secondly, one who is brave; thirdly, one who is clever; fourthly, a chief; fifthly, one who is liberal; sixthly, one possessed of virtuous qualities; and seventhly, one who is a protector of his wife."

The result was that she became pregnant that night, and a son was born. On the sixth night after her delivery, the mother saw in a dream a *Yogi*,[21] on whose head there was matted hair and a shining moon. On his forehead were ashes of cow-dung rubbed over his body. He was wearing a white Brahminical thread, a necklace of white snakes, a garland of skulls, with a skull in one hand and a trident in the other. Having assumed a very frightful form, he came before her and said, "Tomorrow, at midnight, shut in a large basket, and place before the gate of the palace, a purse of a thousand gold mohurs and this boy."

While she was looking at this apparition she awoke. In the early morning she mentioned all the circumstances to her mother. Having heard them, her mother shut the boy in a large basket in the manner pointed out and placed him at the King's door. Now the King also saw in a dream a figure[22] with ten arms, five heads, three eyes in each head, and a moon upon each head and a trident in his hand which said, "King! A basket has been placed at your door; take the child that is in it, he shall maintain your Government."

On hearing this, the King awoke, and then told all the circumstances to his wife. At the door he saw a large basket containing a boy and a thousand gold mohurs. He took up the child himself and placed the child in his wife's lap.

The King sent for the astrologers and asked them to tell him what marks of royalty there were in the child.

One among them, a Brahmin said, "O great king! Three marks[23] are manifestly visible in this child; one large breast, the second, a high forehead, and the third, a large face; and besides these, marks which are common to all men. You may therefore set your mind at rest that he will obtain sovereignty."

The King was delighted at hearing this and, taking a pearl necklace from his neck gave it to that Brahmin. Having made many presents to all the Brahmins, he ordered them to name the child.

Then the pundits said, "O great king! Please sit bound in a knot[24] with your wife. Let the queen sit down with the child in her

[21] This description of the jogee answers precisely to that given of Shiva or Mahadeo, who takes form of a religious mendicant; hence the dream is considered a divine revelation.

[22] These are also distinguishing marks of Shiva.

[23] In one of the quasi-sacred books of the Hindus, there is a long list of the several marks on the human body ("lakshan") with statement of the destiny foreshown by these marks.

lap, and send for musicians and dancers and persons employed at merrymaking, and give festive entertainment, and we will give him a name in the manner prescribed by the Shastras."

When the King heard this, he ordered his minister to do as they said, and the minister immediately caused a proclamation of rejoicing to be made throughout the city on account of the birth of the child. All the people who attend rejoicing came to the King's palace when they heard the proclamation. Congratulations began to pour in from every house, and the musical rejoicing and festivities in the King's palace commenced.

Then the King and Queen, having taken the child, came and sat down in a place filled with sweetmeats. The Brahmins began to read the Vedas. One among the Brahmins, an astrologer, having determined the auspicious planetary aspect, named the child Hardutt.[25]

At the age of nine years, he read the six Shastras and fourteen sciences and became learned. His mother and father died, and he ascended the throne and began to govern justly.

But after many years, the King one day thought to himself that he had done nothing for their sakes. Having reflected and considered, the King thought that he ought now to perform the funeral obsequies of his parents.

Then the King Hardutt went to Gaya. On arriving there, having invoked the names of his parents, he began to offer balls made of flour and rice on the bank of the river, where the hands[26] of three people came forth from the river. He was perplexed when he beheld this, and did not know into whose hands he should give the balls."

Having proceeded this far in the narrative, the Baital said, "King Vikram! To whom of those three was it right to give the balls of flour and rice?"

The King replied, "To the thief."

The Baital enquired the reason, and the King said, "The seed of the Brahmin was purchased, and the King took a thousand gold

---

[24] That is, sit with a long cloth tied round yourself and your wife.

[25] That is given by Har, a name of Shiva or Mahadeo.

[26] It is believed that when sons perform the ceremony of offering "pind" to their deceased fathers, the fathers are permitted to come from the other world and stretch out their hands to receive the offering. Hence the text means that the three fathers claimed the offering of Hardutt, *viz.* the thief to whom his mother was married at the stake, the Brahmin who begat, and the rajah who brought him up.

mohurs and brought up the child. Those two therefore, had no right to the balls of flour and rice."

When the Baital heard this, he went again to the tree and was suspended on it; and the King having bound him, placed him upon his shoulder took him away.

THE NINETEENTH TALE

The Baital said, "King! There is a city named Chitrakut, the King of which was Rupdutt. One day he rode out alone hunting and, having lost his way came into a great forest. There he saw a large tank in which lotuses were in full bloom, and birds of different kinds were sporting in the water.

On all sides of the tank under thick shady trees cool, perfumed breezes were blowing. He, being overcome with the heat and having fastened his horse to a tree, spread out his cloth and sat down upon it. After about a quarter of an hour, a beautiful sage's daughter came there to gather flowers. Seeing her plucking flowers, the King became deeply enamoured.

When she had gathered the flowers she was about to return home, when the King said, "What sort of custom is this that you have not paid any attention to me, who has come to your abode as a guest?"

Upon hearing these words she stood still. The King said, "It is a saying that even if a person of low caste should come into the house of a man of the highest caste, he should deserve respect. And whoever comes into our houses, whether he be a thief, or a man of inferior caste, it is right to offer worship to him, because a guest is the most important man of all the party."

When the King had spoken thus, she looked deeply at him and in the meantime the sage [her father] also arrived.

When the King saw the devotee, he made a reverential salutation, and the sage gave the King a blessing, wishing him long life. Having said this, he asked the King, why he had come here.

He said, "O great sage! I have come here to hunt."

The sage replied, "Why do you commit a great sin? It has been said that one man commits sin and many men enjoy the fruits of the sin."

The King said, "O great sage! Take compassion on me and tell me your opinion of right and wrong."

The sage replied, "Please to listen to me, O great king! It is very wrong to kill animals which eat grass and drink water and dwell in the jungles. It is a very virtuous act in a man to cherish animals and birds. It has been said that they who are respectful of their guests and free from fears obtain the advantages of a very charitable man. There is another saying, that austere devotion is not equal to forgiveness. Pleasure is not equivalent to contentment, or wealth to friendship, nor justice to compassion. Men who are observant of religion, having obtained wealth, good qualities, science, celebrity, and high position, do not indulge in pride. They who are content with their own wives, and are speakers of truth, obtain deliverance hereafter. Those who kill ascetics, men with matted hair who go without clothes and are not warlike, obtain hell hereafter. The King who does not punish those who afflict his subjects also goes to hell. And they, who have sexual connection with a King's wife, or with the wife of a friend, or with a young girl, or with a woman advanced in pregnancy, fall into the great hell. This is what is said in the Dharma Shastra."

Having heard this speech, the King replied, "Whatever sins I may hitherto have committed from ignorance, the Supreme Being willing, I will not commit them again."

The sage being delighted at the King's word said, "I will grant you whatever boon you ask; I have been highly pleased with you."

The King replied, "O great sage! If you are gratified with me, give me your daughter."

When the sage heard this, he married his daughter to the King according to the customs of Gandharb marriages and went home. The King went towards his own city, taking the sage's daughter with him, and when he arrived half way, the sun set and the moon rose.

Then the King, having seen a tree with thick foliage, and having dismounted under it and fastened his horse to the root of it, spread out his saddle cloth, and slept there with her.

About midnight a demon, having come by, awoke the King and said, "King! I will eat your wife."

The King said, "Do not do so, I will give you whatsoever you shall ask."

The demon replied, "King, if you will cut off, with your own hand, the head of a Brahmin's son of seven years of age and give it to me, I will not eat your wife."

The King said, "I will do so, but please come to my city in seven days, and I will give you the head."

Having thus bound the King by a promise, the demon went home, and early in the morning, the King entered his palace. His minister made great rejoicing when he heard of his arrival and came and offered presents. The King, having told him all the circumstances, inquired, "What arrangements shall we make, as the demon will come on the seventh day?"

The minister said, "O great king! Be not anxious, God will do all that is right."

The minister, having thus spoken, had a statue of gold made, weighing a maund and a quarter. He had it studded with jewels, put it on a cart and placed it where four roads met. He said to the keepers of it, "Let any Brahmin, who will allow the King to cut off the head of his seven-year-old son, take away this statue."

When he had thus spoken he came and the watchmen told all the people to look at the statue. Two days passed and, on the third, a weakly Brahmin with three sons who had heard of this affair, came home and said to his wife, "Sacrifice one son to the Rajah and a golden, jeweled statue weighing a maund and a quarter will come into your house."

The Brahmin's wife said, "I will not give the youngest," and the Brahmin said, "I will not give the eldest," but the second son, having heard this, said, "Father! Give me for sacrifice."

The Brahmin agreed and then said, "In this world wealth is the root of everything and how can a man without money be happy? A poor man's coming into the world is profitless."

Having said this, he took his second son and gave him to the watchmen, then brought the statue home. And the people brought the child to the minister.

After seven days had elapsed the demon came. The King, having taken sandal, unbroken rice, flowers, perfumes, lights, consecrated food, fruits, pawn, and dresses, offered the child and taking a sword in his hand, stood up to make the sacrifice.

Upon this the child first laughed and afterwards cried. In the meantime the King gave him a blow with the sword, and his head was severed from his body.

The wise have said that in this world women are a mine of grief and abode of solicitation, the destroyers of resolution and the plunderers of virtuous qualities. Who can call such a root of poison excellent? And it has been said, "Keep your wealth for times of misfortune and spend your wealth to protect your wife. Give wealth and wife to save your own life." "

Having told so much of the story, the Baital said, "King, at the time of dying, a person weeps. Explain the reason why the child laughed."

The King said, "When he laughed he thought that the mother protects her son in childhood and the father when he is grown up. A King assists his subjects in good and bad times; such is the custom of the world. Now this is my state; my mother and father through greed have given me to the King, who with a sword in his hand is ready to kill me. The gods are desirous of a sacrifice and no-one has compassion on me."

Having heard this, the Baital went and was suspended on that tree and the King arrived there quickly and having bound him, placed him upon his shoulder, and took him away.

THE TWENTIETH TALE

The Baital said, "King! There is a city named Vishalpur, of which the King's name was Vipuleshwar. In this city was a trader, named Arthdutt, who had a daughter, named Anangmanjari, whom he married to a trader of Kanwalpur City, named Munni.

After sometime the trader crossed the sea for trading. When Anangmanjari was at the age of puberty, she was standing in the garden and watching what was going on. A Brahmin's son, by the name of Kamalakar, was coming by and their eyes met. On seeing each other, they were both fascinated with each other.

After about a quarter of an hour, having recovered, the Brahmin's son went to his friend's house but was restless at the separation from his sweetheart. She too was in a state of extreme uneasiness from the pangs of absence.

In the meantime a female companion came, for she had lost all recollection. The attendant then sprinkled her with rosewater and perfumes. When she was restored to her senses, she said, "O Kamdeo; (Cupid) Mahadeo has reduced you to ashes[27] and still you do not depart from your perfidy or inflict pain on the weak who have not committed any fault."

As evening came and then looking towards the moon she said, "O moon! I had heard that in you is the water of immortality and that you pour it down from your rays. But today you have also

---

[27] Once when Shiva or Mahadeo was engaged in religious meditation, Kamdeo excited him to lustful amusement and Shiva being angry reduced him to ashes by a glance. Kamdeo, however, reappeared on earth *vide* the fifty-sixth chapter of the English translation of the Prem-Sagar. From having been burnt by Shiva's glance is often termed. Anang, or the unbodied.

began to rain down poison on me." She then said to her companion, "Take me up and carry me away, as I am being burnt to death by the moon beams."

At this the attendant raised her and took her to a shed and said, "Are you not ashamed to talk in this way?"

She replied, "O friend! I am aware of all I have said, but Cupid has struck me and made me shameless. Although I make many efforts to be patient, I am so burnt up by the fire of separation, that home seems to me like prison."

Her companion said, "Be of good cheer, I will dispel all your grief."

Having said this, the attendant went to her own home, and she, the trader's daughter, thought to herself, "I will abandon this body for his sake, and having been born again I will enjoy sexual pleasure with him."

Having formed this desire, she threw a noose over her neck, and was on the point of pulling it tight, when her companion arrived, who immediately removed the rope from her neck, and said, "If we have life, we have everything, but we have naught by dying."

She said, "Death is better then suffering this pain."

The attendant replied, "Rest for a quarter of an hour, while I go and bring him here."

Having thus spoken, she went to Kamalakar but hid concealed from him. He also was greatly agitated by the pain of separation. His friend had mixed sandal with rosewater and was rubbing his body with it, and was fanning him with soft plantain leaves. But instead of this he was still burnt up by the pains of separation. He exclaimed to his friend, "Bring me poison, and I will escape from this affliction by relinquishing life."

Seeing him in this state, she said to herself, "However resolute, learned, clever, discreet, or brave a man may be, Cupid will reduce him to a state of distraction in a second." With these thoughts in her mind, the attendant said to him, "O Kumulakar! Anangmanjari tells you to come to her and give her life."

He said, "She has restored me to life." Having said this, he rose up and the attendant, having taken him with her, came to Anangamanjari. On arriving there he saw her lying on the ground dead, and he heaved a deep sigh and his life also immediately departed.

Early in the morning the people of the house carried off both of them to the place where their bodies were burnt. Having erected a funeral pyre, they placed them on it and kindled it.

In the meantime, her husband came from a foreign country to the place where bodies were being burnt, and, having heard the sound of people crying went there and saw that his wife was being burnt with a strange man. Being greatly distressed at being separated from the one he loved, he burnt himself that instant and expired.

Having narrated this much of the story the Baital said, "Which of these three, O King, was most in love?"

The King replied, "Her husband."

And the Baital inquired the reason, "Why?"

The King said, "He who saw the wife had sacrificed her life for another man's sake, and laying aside all anger, being deeply in love with her, gave up his life for her sake. He was the most in love."

Having heard this, the Baital returned to the tree and was suspended on it; the King also went there and having bound him, placed him upon his shoulder, and took him away.

THE TWENTY-FIRST TALE

The Baital said, "King! There is a city named Jaysthal, the King of which is Bradhaman. Now in this city was a Brahmin named Vishnu Swami, who had four sons, one a gambler, the second a whore-monger, the third a fornicator with low strumpets and the fourth an atheist.

One day the Brahmin began to explain to his sons that wealth does not remain in the house of the gambler. When the gambler heard this, he was greatly troubled in mind.

The Brahmin said, "It is written thus in the Rajnit,[28] cut off a gambler's nose and ears and remove him from the country, in order that other men may not gamble. Even though a gambler's wife and children may be in the house, do not consider them as being there, because it is not known when he may lose them. And they who are fascinated by the behavior of prostitutes, purchase grief for their own minds, and being in the power of harlots, give to them all their property, and at last commit theft. It has also been said that the wise keep faraway from a woman, who can fascinate a man's mind in a quarter of an hour. The ignorant, forming affection for her, forfeit their true good disposition. The advice of their spiritual preceptors is not agreeable to them."

And he said, "Why should a man who had lost all shame for himself fear to disgrace another? A proverb says, "when will a wild cat that devours its own young lets a rat go?" He went on to say, "They who do not read science in their youth are distracted by love. They who have remained in the pride of youth, feel regret in their old age and are burnt in the fire of greed."

[28] Name of a Hindi work on the science of government.

Having heard these words, the four young men reflected amongst themselves and said, "It is better to die than live as a man without science, and therefore it is best that we go into another country and study science." Having formed this resolution, the four went to another city and having studied for sometime, became learned and returned home.

On the road they saw a Kanjar[29] who had separated the bones and skin of a tiger and was on the point of taking them away in a bundle. On this they said to each other, "Let us come and test our science."

So one of them called the Kanjar and gave him something and having taken his bundle, allowed him to depart. One of them opened the bundle. Having arranged all the bones in their proper places, he read an incantation and sprinkled them with water. The bones then adhered together. The second in like manner collected and placed the flesh upon the bones. The third placed the skin upon the bones in the same way, and the fourth in a similar manner gave life to the animal. Upon this, the tiger rose up and devoured all four of them."

Having related this much of the story, the Baital said, "Who was the greatest fool of the four?"

King Vikram said, "The one who gave life to the tiger was the greatest fool. It has been said, "Science is useless without understanding; understanding is better than science and they who are devoid of understanding die, just as they who brought the tiger to life again died.'"

Having heard these words, the Baital went to the tree, and was suspended on it; and the King having fastened him, placed him upon his shoulder and took him away again.

[29] A particular caste that catch and exhibit snakes and perform mean offices.

THE TWENTY-SECOND TALE

The Baital said, "King, there was a city named Vishapur, the King of which was named Bidagdh. In this city was a Brahmin named Narayan.

One day he began to think to himself, "My body has become old. As I understand the power of entering into another person's body, it is better for me to abandon this old body and enter into the body of some youth, and enjoy sexual pleasure."

When he had thus reflected he began to enter into a youthful body he first wept and then laughed. Having entered into the body, he came home but all his relations knew what he had done. He began to say in their presence, that he was a yogi.

Having thus spoken, he began, "He may be called a wise yogi who has dried up the reservoir of hope with the fire of austere devotion. He is a yogi who has subdued his own mind and kept the organs of the senses in their proper places. When men's bodies are old, they begin to dissolve, their heads shake and their teeth fall out. They walk about with sticks, but even at this time of life greed is not affected. Old age succeeds childhood and we know not who we are. At last all living creatures must depart. There are bodies and minds of many kinds. Brahma has created wickedness of many kinds. Some wise men have escaped hope and avarice. They, having shaven their heads, taken a stick and waterpot in their hands and having subjugated the passion of love and anger, have become yogis. They wander and travel about with naked feet to places of pilgrimage and obtain final liberation in this world like a dream. Whoever you may please and whomever you may lament, the world is like the leaves springing from the center of the plantain. The world has no value and they who pride themselves on wealth, youth and science, are unwise. They who become religious devotees then ask for alms and nourishment for their bodies with milk and sugar. Those who fall in love and indulge in voluptuous pleasure with women destroy their religious devotion. They lose all the advantages desirable from it."

Having read this much, he said, "I will now go on pilgrimage." When his relations heard this, they were greatly pleased."

Having told so much of the story, the Baital said, "King! Why did he weep, and why did he laugh?"

The King replied, "He wept when he recalled the affection of his mother in childhood and from this feeling of affection that had remained so many days in that body. He laughed when he had brought his power to a successful conclusion and entered the new body."

Having heard this, the Baital went to that tree and was suspended on it; and the King took him away, and having bound him placed him upon his shoulder in the same manner as before, and went away.

THE TWENTY-THIRD TALE

The Baital said, "King! There was a city named Dharampur, the King of which was Dharamraj. In this city was a Brahmin named Govind, versed in the four Vedas and six Shastras, and attentive to all religious observances. And he had four sons, Haridutt, Somdutt, Jaggadutt and Brahmdutt, who were very learned, very wise, and constantly obedient to the commands of their father.

After sometime his eldest son died. The father was on the point of death from affliction at his loss when the family priest, by name Vishnu Sharma, came and said, "Man, from the time he comes into his mother's womb, suffers pain. In youth, being subdued by love, he is distressed at being separated from her he loves. When he becomes an old man, his body becoming weak afflicts him. In short, the condition of being born brings much grief and few pleasures, because this world is the root of misery.

At the most man's age is a hundred years, half of which passes away at night. The other half is expended in childhood and old age; the remainder is spent in altercation, separation from those we love, and affliction, and the soul is as restless as a wave of the sea. What happiness, therefore, has man? And now in the black age, men who are speakers of the truth are few. Kings have become avaricious, the earth brings forth fewer fruits, thieves and irreligious men commit acts of violence, and there is little religion, austere devotion, or truth left in the world.

Death did not spare Abhimanyu, whose maternal uncle was Krishna and father Arjun and whenever Yama[30] carries off a mortal

[30] Answers in many respects to the Pluto of the Greek-Mythology. He is the regent of death, or rather death personified, and rules over the infernal regions.

body his wealth remains behind. And behold! Night passes away, and then day dawns; the moon goes down, and the sun rises. Thus does youth depart and old age comes on, and thus time pursues its course. Still man sees all these things, but he does not become wise. And behold! In the virtuous age Mandhata was so great that he spread over the whole earth with the fame of his justice and religion. No one, who has come into the world, has escaped from affliction. It is vain to fix one's affections on it; and, therefore, it is best to cultivate and practise religion."

When Vishnu Sharma had entered into this explanation it occurred to the Brahmin, that he ought to perform virtuous and charitable acts. With this thought in mind, he said to his sons, "I will sit down to offer sacrifice; go and bring me a tortoise from the sea."

Hearing their father's order, they went to a fisherman, and said, "Take a rupee and catch a tortoise for us." He took the money and caught a tortoise and gave it to them.

Upon this, the elder brother told the youngest, who said, "I will not touch it, as an unpleasant smell will come upon my hands. I am skilled in eating."

The second said "I am skilful in keeping or entertaining women," and the eldest said, "I have skill in sleeping on beds of different kinds." The three began to dispute and having left the tortoise there, went quarrelling along the road to the King's gate, and said to the doorkeeper, "Go and tell the King that three Brahmins have come to make a complaint."

When the doorkeeper heard this, he went and informed the King. The brothers came and the first one said, "O great king! I am skilled in the refinements of food. The second said, "O lord of the earth! I am skilled in knowing woman."

The eldest said, "O incarnation of justice! I have skill in beds."

When the King had heard this, he ordered each to exhibit a proof of his skill, and they agreed to do so. The King sent for his cook and told him to prepare condiment and dishes for the Brahmin. The cook, having heard this, placed it before him food. But the food smelled badly, so he left it and, having washed his hands, came to the King, who asked him if he had enjoyed the meal.

He said "O great king! I did not eat the food, because the rice had been produced on a burial ground, and it smelt of corpses."

The King having heard this sent for his house steward and enquired, "From which village did this rice come?"

And the steward from, "From Shivpur."

The King told him to call the head landholder of the village to be summoned into his presence, and the King enquired, "From what land has this rice been produced?" He replied, "From cemetery land."

When the King heard this, he said to the Brahmin's son, "You truly have a delicate taste in food."

He then called the one who was skilled in women. A bed was prepared in a room and, having made the most pleasing and voluptuous preparations, he summoned a beautiful woman. The King had her placed by the Brahmin's side and reclining on the bed they began to converse with each other.

The King, who was concealed, began to look through a lattice. And the Brahmin was on the point of kissing her when, smelling her breath, he turned away his face and went to sleep.

When the Rajah saw this conduct on the part of the Brahmin, he returned to his palace and retired for the night. Early in the morning, having risen and come into his court, the King sent for the Brahmin and enquired, "Brahmin! Did you pass the night pleasantly?"

He said, "O great King! I did not enjoy any pleasure."

The King asked the reason and the Brahmin said, 'The smell of goat came from her mouth, and I was very uneasy, and dissatisfied in consequence."

The King having heard this enquired, "Who was the woman?"

She said, "This is my sister's daughter, whose mother died when the child was three years of age, and I have nourished her, and brought her up on goat's milk.

When the King heard this, he told the Brahmin that he was skilled in knowing women.

He the called for the Brahmin who was skilled in the qualities of different kinds of beds, and he was placed on a bed. At dawn the next day the King sent for him, and enquired whether he had slept comfortably.

He said, "O great king! I did not sleep all night."

The King asked, "Why?" and he said, "O great king! In the seventh fold of this bedding there is a hair, which pricked me in the back, and therefore I could not sleep."

The Rajah having heard this, looked at the seventh fold of bedding and saw a hair barely visible there, and said to the Brahmin, "You are indeed acquainted with the different qualities of beds." "

Having proceeded this far in the narrative the Baital enquired, "Who was the most intelligent and cleverest of the three?"

And the King Vir Vikramaditya said, "The one who was acquainted with the different kinds of beds, because his skill was so sensitive."

Having heard this, the Baital went again to the tree, and was suspended on it; and the King went there also immediately, and having bound him placed him upon his shoulder, and took him away.

THE TWENTY-FOURTH TALE

The Baital said, "King! In the Kalinga country there was a Brahmin, named Jaggasharma, whose wife, named Somdatta, was exceedingly beautiful.

The Brahmin began to offer sacrifice and, in consequence thereof, his wife had a pretty son. When the child was five years of age, his father began to instruct him in the Shastra. By the age of twelve years, he became very learned and began to serve his father.

After the lapse of some time, the son died and his mother and father began to shed tears and pour forth loud lamentations. All their relatives hastened to their house when they heard the news. After they had arrived there, they remarked to each other that he appeared beautiful even in death.

While they were so engaged, a religious devotee, having heard their conversation, said to himself, "My own body has become very old and if I were to enter the body of the child, I could perform penance with pleasure."

Having thus reflected, he entered into the child's body and, calling upon the name of Ram Krishna, he rose and sat up. All the people were astonished when they saw this and they returned home, but the father, having seen this strange sight, became a religious devotee, and abandoned all the pleasures of the world. He first laughed and then wept."

Having related this much of the story the Baital said, "King Vikramaditya; say why he laughed, and why he cried?"

The King replied, "He laughed at seeing the devotee enter his son's body and he wept from regret at having to quit his own body, thinking that it would be his fate to abandon his own body in a like manner."

Having heard this, the Baital went again to the tree, and was suspended on it; and the King went after him, and having fastened him placed him upon his shoulder and took him away.

THE TWENTY-FIFTH TALE

Then the Baital said, "King, in the Deccan country is the city of Dharampur, the King of which was named Mahabal.

Once upon a time another King of that country came and attacked him with an army and encompassed his city. The King continued fighting for many days, but when he was reduced to despair he went forth at night to the jungle, taking his wife and daughter with him.

When they had travelled some way in the forest, day dawned and a village appeared in sight. The King, having seated his wife and daughter under a tree, went himself towards the village to bring something to eat, when some Bhils came and surrounded him, and told him to throw down his arms.

Having heard this, the King began discharging arrows. The fight continued in this way for three hours, and many of the Bhils were killed. In the meantime an arrow struck the skull of the King with such force that he fell down and a Bhil came and cut off his head.

When the queen and her daughter saw that the King was dead, they returned to the forest, weeping and striking their breasts. They became weary and sat down, and began to indulge in anxious reflections and thoughts of various kinds.

In the meantime a King named Chandarsen, and his son, were hunting in the jungle. The King happened to see the marks of the two women's feet, and said to his son, "From where have the marks of the mortal feet made their appearance?"

The son said, "O great king, these are the marks of women feet, a man's foot would not be so small."

The King replied, "Certainly such a soft delicate foot cannot be a man's."

The son said, "They have only just passed by."

The King said "Come, let us look for them in this forest. If we find them, I will give you the one whose foot is larger, and I will take the other one myself."

Having made this agreement, and proceeded on their road, they saw them both sitting down. Delighted at seeing them, the King and his son seated the ladies according to agreement on their horses, and brought them home; the son kept the mother, and the father, the daughter."

Having proceeded this far in the narrative the Baital said, "King Vikramaditya! What relationship will have there been between the sons of these two?"

Having heard this, the King being ignorant, replied silent.

The Baital pleased again said, "King! I have been highly delighted at beholding your firmness and resolution but listen to one thing I am about to tell you.

A man has come into your city, the hairs on his body are like thorns, and his body like wood, and his name is Shantshil. He has sent you to bring me; he is himself sitting in a cemetery, and performing incantations, and he wishes to kill you. Therefore I put you on your guard, that when he shall have finished his prayers, he will say to you, "King! Make a prostration, so that the eight principal parts of your body may touch the ground."

Then do you say, "I am the King of all Kings. All Kings come and make salutation to me and hitherto I have not made a salutation to anyone, and know not how to do so. You are a spiritual preceptor, be pleased to do me the favour to instruct me, and I will do what you wish. When he makes the salutation, inflict on him such a wound with your sword, that his head many be severed from his body and then you shall enjoy an unbroken reign. If you do not do this, he will kill you, and his power will be immovably established."

Having thus cautioned the King, the Baital came forth from the dead body, and took his departure; and the King brought the corpse and placed it before the devotee (yogi) who, on seeing it, was pleased and greatly extolled the King.

Then having pronounced some incantations and awakened the dead man, he offered up a sacrifice and being seated facing to the south, he offered up to his Deity all the different prayers. Having given offerings of flowers, perfumes, lamps and consecrated food, and said prayers; he addressed the King thus. "You must make prostration to me, you will obtain great splendour and glory. Wealth and treasures of all kinds shall remain for ever in your house, and all your wishes shall be accomplished."

The King heard these words and recollected what the Baital had said to him. He answered with joined hands and greatest humility, "O great king! I know not how to perform prostration, but you are a spiritual preceptor, and if you will do me the favour to instruct me, I will make one."

When the devotee, having heard this bent his head to make salutation, the King struck him a blow with his sword, and his head was severed from his body, and the Baital came and rained down flowers.

Thus it has been said, "That there is no injustice in killing a man who is about to kill himself or who wishes to kill himself."[31]

At that time Indra and all the gods, having seen the King's courage seated in their chariots, began to raise shouts of victory and exultation. Indra, being delighted with King Vikramaditya, said to him, "Ask a boon."

Then the King, having joined his hands, said, "O great king, let this my history be published in the world."

Indra replied, "This history shall be generally known so long as the moon, sun, earth, and sky continue and you shall be King of the whole world."

Having thus spoken, Indra departed to his own abode, and the King, having taken those corpses, threw them into that cauldron of oil. Then these two heroes made their appearance, and said, "What are your commands for us?"

The King, "Come, when I call you."

Having exacted this promise from them, the King went home, and began to administer the affairs of his government. There is a saying, "That man, being learned or a fool, a child or a youth, if he be possessed of intellect and mind, will triumph and obtain preferment."

[31] The meaning is that if A, be attempting to slay B. B. is justified in killing A.

MORE FOLKTALES FROM PILGRIMS PUBLISHING

[illegible]

PILGRIMS BOOK HOUSE

[illegible]